The Woman in the Dunes

Translated from the Japanese by

E. DALE SAUNDERS

With drawings by

MACHI ABÉ

The Woman
in the Dunes

BY KOBO ABÉ

✹ VINTAGE BOOKS
A Division of Random House, New York

Copyright © 1964 by Alfred A. Knopf, Inc.

All rights reserved under International and Pan-American
Copyright Conventions. Published in the United States by
Random House, Inc., New York, and simultaneously in
Canada by Random House of Canada Limited, Toronto.
Originally published in the United States by Alfred A.
Knopf, Inc., in 1964.

Originally published in Japanese by Shinchosha as
Suna no Onna.

Library of Congress Cataloging in Publication Data

Abé, Kobo, 1924-
   The woman in the dunes.

   Translation of Suna no onna.
   I. Title.
[PZ4.A13Wo 5]   [PL845.B4]   895.6'3'5   72-764
ISBN 0-394-71814-3

Manufactured in the United States of America

Vintage Books Edition, September 1972

WITHOUT THE THREAT
OF PUNISHMENT
THERE IS NO JOY
IN FLIGHT

PART I

1

~~~~~~~~~~~~~~~~~~~~~~~~

One day in August a man disappeared. He had simply set out for the seashore on a holiday, scarcely half a day away by train, and nothing more was ever heard of him. Investigation by the police and inquiries in the newspapers had both proved fruitless.

Of course, missing persons are not really uncommon. According to the statistics, several hundred disappearances are reported every year. Moreover, the proportion of those found again is unexpectedly small. Murders or accidents always leave some clear piece of evidence, and the motives for kidnapping are normally ascertainable. But if the instance does not come under some such heading, clues—and this is especially true in the case of missing persons—are extremely difficult to come by. Many disappearances, for example, may be described as simple escape.

In the case of this man, also, the clues were negligible.

Though his general destination was known, there had been no report from the area that a body had been discovered. By its very nature, it was inconceivable that his work involved some secret for which he might have been abducted. His quite normal behavior had not given the slightest hint that he intended to vanish.

Naturally, everyone at first imagined that a woman was involved. But his wife, or at least the woman he lived with, announced that the object of his trip had been to collect insect specimens. The police investigators and his colleagues felt vaguely disappointed. The insect bottle and net were hardly a feint for a runaway trip with a girl. Then, too, a station employee at S—— had remembered a man getting off the train who looked like a mountain climber and carried slung across his shoulders a canteen and a wooden box, which he took to be a painting set. The man had been alone, quite alone, the employee said, so speculation about a girl was groundless.

The theory had been advanced that the man, tired of life, had committed suicide. One of his colleagues, who was an amateur psychoanalyst, held to this view. He claimed that in a grown man enthusiasm for such a useless pastime as collecting insects was evidence enough of a mental quirk. Even in children, unusual preoccupation with insect collecting frequently indicates an Oedipus complex. In order to compensate for his unsatisfied desires, the child enjoys sticking pins into insects, which he need never fear will escape. And the fact that he does not leave off once he has grown up is quite definitely a sign that the condition has become worse. Thus it is far from accidental that entomol-

ogists frequently have an acute desire for acquisitions and that they are extremely reclusive, kleptomaniac, homosexual. From this point to suicide out of weariness with the world is but a step. As a matter of fact, there are even some collectors who are attracted by the potassium cyanide in their bottles rather than by the collecting itself, and no matter how they try they are quite incapable of washing their hands of the business. Indeed, the man had not once confided his interests to anyone, and this would seem to be proof that he realized they were rather dubious.

Yet, since no body had actually been discovered, all of these ingenious speculations were groundless.

Seven years had passed without anyone learning the truth, and so, in compliance with Section 30 of the civil code, the man had been pronounced dead.

2

~~~~~~~~~~~~~~~~~

ONE August afternoon a man stood in the railroad station at S——. He wore a gray peaked hat, and the cuffs of his trousers were tucked into his stockings. A canteen and a large wooden box were slung over his shoulders. He seemed about to set out on a mountain-climbing expedition.

Yet there were no mountains worth climbing in the immediate vicinity. Indeed, the guard who took his ticket at the gate looked at him quizzically after he passed through.

The man showed no hesitancy as he entered the bus standing in front of the station and took a seat in the back. The bus route led away from the mountains.

The man stayed on the bus to the end of the run. When he got off, the landscape was a mixture of hillocks and hollows. The lowlands were rice paddies that had been divided into narrow strips, while among them slightly elevated fields planted with persimmon trees were scattered about like islands. The man passed through a village and continued walking in the direction of the seashore; the soil gradually became whitish and dry.

After a time there were no more houses, only straggling clumps of pine. Then the soil changed to a fine sand that clung to his feet. Now and again clumps of dry grass cast shadows in hollows in the sand. As if by mistake, there was occasionally a meager plot of eggplants, the size of a straw mat. But of human shadows there was not a trace. The sea, toward which he was headed, lay beyond.

For the first time the man stopped. He wiped the perspiration from his face with his sleeve and gazed around. With deliberation, he opened the wooden box and from the top drawer took out several pieces of pole that had been bundled together. He assembled them into a handle and attached an insect net to one end. Then he began to walk again, striking the clumps of grass with the bottom of the shaft. The smell of the sea enveloped the sands.

Some time went by, but the sea still could not be seen. Perhaps the hilly terrain obstructed the view. The unchanging landscape stretched endlessly on. Then, suddenly, the perspective broadened and a hamlet came into sight. It was a commonplace, rather poor village, whose roofs, weighted down with stones, lay clustered around a high fire tower. Some of the roofs were shingled with black tile; others were of zinc, painted red. A zinc-roofed building at the hamlet's single crossroad seemed to be the meeting house of a fishermen's cooperative.

Beyond, there were probably more dunes, and the sea. Still, the hamlet was spread out to an unexpected extent. There were some fertile patches, but the soil consisted mostly of dry white sand. There were fields of potatoes and peanuts, and the odor of domestic animals mingled with that of the sea. A pile of broken shells formed a white mound at the side of the clay-and-sand road, which was as hard as cement. As the man passed down the street, children were playing in the empty lot in front of the cooperative, some old men were sitting on the sagging veranda repairing their nets, and thin-haired women were gathered in front of the single general store. All movement ceased for a moment as they looked curiously at him. But the man paid no attention. Sand and insects were all that concerned him.

However, the size of the village was not the only surprising thing. Contrary to what one would expect, the road was gradually rising. Since it led toward the sea, it would be more natural for it to descend. Could he have misread the map? He tried questioning a young village girl who was passing by just then. But she lowered her eyes and, acting as if she had not heard a thing, hurried on. Yet the pile of shells, the fishing nets, and the color of the sand told him that certainly the sea lay nearby. There was really nothing yet that foretold danger.

The road began to rise more and more abruptly; more and more it became just sand.

But, curiously enough, the areas where houses stood were not the slightest bit higher. The road alone rose, while the hamlet itself continued to remain level. No, it was not only the road; the areas between the buildings were rising at the same rate. In a sense, then, the whole village seemed to have become a rising slope with only the buildings left on their original level. This impression became more striking as he went along. At length, all the houses seemed to be sunk into hollows scooped in the sand. The surface of the sand stood higher than the rooftops. The successive rows of houses sank deeper and deeper into the depressions.

The slope suddenly steepened. It must have been at least sixty-five feet down to the tops of the houses. What in heaven's name could it be like to live there? he thought in amazement, peering down into one of the holes. As he circled around the edge he was suddenly struck by a biting wind that choked his breath in his throat. The view abruptly opened up, and the turbid, foaming sea licked at the shore below. He was standing on the crest of the dunes that had been his objective!

The side of the dunes that faced the sea and received the monsoon winds rose abruptly, but straggling clumps of scrub grass grew in places where the incline was not as steep. The man looked back over his shoulder at the village, and he could see that the great holes, which grew deeper as they approached the crest of the ridge, extended in several ranks toward the center. The village, resembling the cross-section of a beehive, lay sprawled over the dunes. Or rather the dunes lay sprawled over the village. Either way, it was a disturbing and unsettling landscape.

But it was enough that he had reached his destination, the dunes. The man drank some water from his canteen and filled his lungs with air—and the air which had seemed so clear felt rough in his throat.

The man intended to collect insects that lived in the dunes.

Of course, dune insects are small and soberly colored. But he was a dedicated collector, and his eye was not tempted by anything like butterflies or dragonflies. Such collectors do not aspire to decking out their specimen boxes with gaudy samples, nor are they particularly interested in classification or in raw materials for Chinese medicines. The true entomologist's pleasure is much simpler, more direct: that of discovering a new type. When this happens, the discover's name appears in the illustrated encyclopedias of entomology appended to the technical Latin name of the newly found insect; and there, perhaps, it is preserved for something less than eternity. His efforts are crowned with success if his name is perpetuated in the memory of his fellow men by being associated with an insect.

The smaller, unobtrusive insects, with their innumerable strains, offer many opportunities for new discoveries. For a long time the man had also been on the lookout for double-winged flies, especially common house flies, which people find so repulsive. Of course, the various types of flies are unbelievably numerous, and since all entomologists seem to think pretty much alike, they have pursued their investigations into the eighth rare mutant found in Japan almost to completion. Perhaps mutants are so abundant because the fly's environment is too close to man's.

He had best begin by observing environment. That there were many environmental variations simply indicated a high degree of adaptability among flies, didn't it? At this discovery he jumped with joy. His concept might not be altogether bad. The fact that the fly showed great adaptability meant that it could be at home even in unfavorable environments in which other insects could not live—for example, a desert where all other living things perished.

From then on he began to manifest an interest in sand. And soon this interest bore fruit. One day in the dry river bed near his house he discovered a smallish light-pink insect which resembled a double-winged garden beetle (*Cicindela japonica* Motschulsky). It is common knowledge, of course, that the garden beetle presents many variations in color and design. But the form of the front legs, on the other hand, varies very little. In fact, the front legs of the sheath-wing beetle constitute an important criterion for its classification. And the second joint on the front legs of the insect that had caught the man's eye did indeed have striking characteristics.

Generally speaking, the front legs of the beetle family are black, slender, and agile. However, the front legs of this one seemed to be covered with a stout sheath; they were round, almost chubby, and cream-colored. Of course, they may have been smeared with pollen. One might even assume some sort of condition—the presence of hair, for example—which would cause the pollen to adhere to the legs. If his observations were correct he had certainly made a most important discovery.

But unfortunately he had let it escape. He had been too excited, and besides the beetle's pattern of flight was confusing. It flew away, and then as if to say "Catch me!" it turned and waited. When he approached it cautiously it flew away again, turned around, and waited. Mercilessly tantalizing, its course had at last led it to a clump of grass into which it disappeared.

The man was completely captivated by the beetle with the yellowish front legs.

When he had observed the sandy soil, it seemed to him that his guess was correct. Actually, the beetle family is representative of desert insects. According to one theory, their strange pattern of flight is a snare for the purpose of enticing small animals away from their nests. Prey such as mice and lizards are lured out in spite of themselves, wander into the desert, and collapse from hunger and fatigue. Their bodies then become the beetles' food. These beetles have the elegant Japanese name of "letter-bearer" and present graceful features, but actually they have sharp jaws and are ferocious and cannibalistic by nature. But whether or not his theory was correct, the man was unquestionably beguiled by the mysterious pattern of the beetle's flight.

And his interest in sand, which was the condition for the beetle's existence, could not help but grow. He began to read everything he could about it. And as his research progressed he realized that sand was a very interesting substance. For example, opening to the article on sand in the encyclopedia, he found the following:

SAND: an aggregate of rock fragments. Sometimes including loadstone, tinstone, and more rarely gold dust. Diameter: 2 to $\frac{1}{16}$ mm.

A very clear definition indeed. In short, then, sand came from fragmented rock and was intermediate between clay and pebbles. But simply calling it an intermediate substance did not provide a really satisfactory explanation. Why was it that isolated deserts and sandy terrain came into existence through the sifting out of only the sand from soil in which clay, sand, and stones were thoroughly mixed together? If a true intermediate substance were involved, the erosive action of wind and water would necessarily produce any number of intermingling intermediate forms in the range between rock and clay. However, there are in fact only three forms that can be clearly distinguished from one another: stones, sand, and clay. Furthermore, sand is sand wherever it is; strangely enough, there is almost no difference in the size of the grains whether they come from the Gobi Desert or from the beach at Enoshima. The size of the grains shows very little variation and follows a Gaussian distribution curve with a true mean of 1/8 mm.

One commentary gave a very simple explanation of the decomposition of land through the erosive action of wind and water: the lighter particles were progressively blown away over great distances. But the particular significance of the 1/8-mm. diameter of the grains was left unexplained. In opposition to this, another book on geology added an explanation along these lines:

Air or water currents set up a turbulence. The smallest wavelength of this turbulent flow is about equal to the diameter of the desert sand. Owing to this peculiarity, only the sand is extracted from the soil, being drawn out at right angles to the flow. If the cohesion of the soil is weak, the sand is sucked up into the air by light winds—which, of course, do not disturb stones or clay—and falls to the ground again, being deposited to the leeward. The peculiarities of sand would seem to be a matter of aerodynamics.

Hence, we can add this to the first definition as "b":

a particle of crushed rock of such dimension as to be easily moved by a fluid.

Because winds and water currents flow over the land, the formation of sand is unavoidable. As long as the winds blew, the rivers flowed, and the seas stirred, sand would be born grain by grain from the earth, and like a living being it would creep everywhere. The sands never rested. Gently but surely they invaded and destroyed the surface of the earth.

This image of the flowing sand made an indescribably exciting impact on the man. The barrenness of sand, as it is usually pictured, was not caused by simple dryness, but apparently was due to the ceaseless movement that made it inhospitable to all living things. What a difference compared with the dreary way human beings clung together year in year out.

Certainly sand was not suitable for life. Yet, was a stationary condition absolutely indispensable for existence? Didn't unpleasant competition arise precisely because one tried to cling to a fixed position? If one were to give up a fixed position and abandon oneself to the movement of the sands, competition would soon stop. Actually, in the deserts flowers bloomed and insects and other animals lived their lives. These creatures were able to escape competition through their great ability to adjust—for example, the man's beetle family.

While he mused on the effect of the flowing sands, he was seized from time to time by hallucinations in which he himself began to move with the flow.

3

His head bent down, he began to walk, following the crescent-shaped line of dunes that surrounded the village like a rampart and towered above it. He paid almost no attention to the distant landscape. An entomologist must concentrate his whole attention within a radius of about three yards around his feet. And it is one of the fundamental rules that he should not have the sun at his back. If the sun should get behind him, he would frighten the insects with his own shadow. As a result, a collector's forehead and nose are always sunburned.

The man advanced slowly at a steady pace. With every step the sand splashed up over his shoes. Except for shallow-rooted weeds that looked as though they would shoot up in a day if there were any moisture, there appeared to be no living thing. Once in a long while, tortoise-shell-colored flies would flit around, drawn by the odor of human perspiration. However, precisely because it was such a place, he could expect to find something. Beetles are not especially gregarious, and they say that, in extreme cases, a single beetle will cordon off an area of as much as one square mile. Patiently, he kept walking round and round.

Suddenly he paused in his tracks. Something had stirred near the roots of a clump of grass. It was a spider. Spiders were of no use to him. He sat down to smoke a cigarette. The wind blew ceaselessly from the sea and, far below, turbulent white waves beat against the base of the sand dunes. Where the dunes fell away to the west a slight hill crowned with bare rock jutted out into the sea. On it the sunshine lay scattered in needlepoints of light.

He had difficulty getting his matches to light. Out of ten tries not one had caught. Along the length of the match-sticks he had thrown away, ripples of sand were moving at about the speed of the second hand of his watch. He focused his attention on one wavelet, and when it arrived at the tip of his heel he arose. The sand spilled from the gathers in his trousers. He spat, and the inside of his mouth felt rough.

So probably there weren't too many insects. Perhaps the movement of the sand was too violent. No, he shouldn't be so quickly discouraged; his theory guaranteed that there would be some.

The line of dunes leveled off, and a section jutted out on the side away from the sea. He was lured on by the feeling that in all probability his prey was there, and he made his way down the gentle slope. Here and there the remains of what seemed like a wind fence made of wattling marked off the point of the promontory, beyond which, on a still lower level, lay a plateau. He went on, cutting across the ripples of sand, which were hewn with machine-like regularity. Suddenly his line of vision was cut off, and he stood on the verge of a cliff looking down into a deep cavity.

The cavity, over sixty feet wide, formed an irregular oval. The far slope seemed relatively gentle, while in contrast the near side gave the feeling of being almost perpendicular. It rolled up to his feet in a smooth curve, like a lip of heavy porcelain. Placing one foot gingerly on the edge, he peered in. The shadowy interior of the hole, set against the luminous edge, already announced the approach of evening.

In the gloom at the bottom a small house lay submerged in silence. One end of its ridgepole was sunk diagonally into the sand wall. Quite like an oyster, he thought.

No matter what they did, he mused, there was no escaping the law of the sand.

Just as he was placing his camera in position, the sand at his feet began to move with a rustle. He drew his foot back, shuddering, but the flow of the sand did not stop for some time. What a delicate, dangerous balance! Breathing deeply, he wiped his sweaty palms several times on the sides of his trousers.

A coughing broke out next to him. Unnoticed, an old man, apparently one of the village fishermen, was standing there almost touching his shoulder. As he looked at the camera and then at the bottom of the hole, the old fellow grinned, screwing up his face, which was wrinkled like a half-tanned rabbit skin. A sticky secretion encrusted the corners of his reddened eyes.

"Are you inspecting?"

It was a thin voice, blown by the wind, rather as if it came from a portable radio. But the accent was clear and not particularly difficult to catch.

"Inspecting?" Flustered, he concealed the lens with his palm. He shifted his insect net into full view. "What do you mean? I don't understand. I'm collecting insects. My specialty is sand insects."

"What?" The old man did not seem to have understood.

"Collecting insects," he repeated again in a loud voice. "Insects. In-sects. I catch them like this!"

"Insects?"

The old man appeared dubious. Looking down, he spat. Or perhaps it would be more exact to say he let the spittle ooze from his mouth. Snatched from his lips by the wind, it sailed out in a long thread. Good heavens, what was he so nervous about?

"Is there some inspecting going on in this vicinity?"

"No, no. As long as you're not inspecting, I really don't mind what you do."

"No, I'm not inspecting."

The old man, without even nodding, turned his back and, scuffing the tips of his straw sandals, went slowly away along the ridge.

Some fifty yards further on—when had they come?—three men dressed alike, apparently waiting for the old man, squatted silently on the sand. The one in the middle had a pair of binoculars, which he was turning around and around on his knee. Soon the three, joined by the old man, began to discuss something among themselves. They kicked the sand at their feet. It looked as if they were having a violent argument.

Just as he was trying unconcernedly to go on with his search for the beetle, the old man came hurrying back again.

"Then you're really not someone from the government office?"

"The government office? You're quite wrong."

Abruptly he took out his business card, as if to indicate that he had had enough. The old man's lips moved laboriously.

"Ah! You're a schoolteacher!"

"I have absolutely no connection with the government office."

"Hmm. So you're a teacher."

At last he appeared to understand, and the corners of his eyes wrinkled up. Carrying the card respectfully, he went back again. The three others, apparently satisfied, stood up and withdrew.

But the old man returned once again.

"By the way, what do you intend doing now?"

"Well, I'm going to look for insects."

"But the last bus back has already gone."

"Isn't there any place I can stay here?"

"Stay all night? In this village?" The man's face twitched.

"If I can't stay here, I'll walk on to the next village."

"Walk?"

"As a matter of fact, I'm in no special hurry."

"Well, why go to all that trouble?" He suddenly became loquacious. "You can see this is a poor village," he said in an accommodating tone. "There isn't a decent house in it, but if it's all right with you I'll put in a good word and see what I can do to help you out."

He did not seem to bear any ill will. They were just being cautious—perhaps on the lookout for some prefectural official who was scheduled to come on a tour of inspection. With their sense of caution appeased, they were merely good, simple fisherfolk.

"I should be very grateful if you would. Of course, I will expect to show my appreciation. . . . I am particularly fond of staying in village houses."

4

~~~~~~~~~~~~~~~~~~~~~~~~

THE sun had set and the wind had slackened somewhat. He walked along the dunes until he could no longer distinguish the pattern hewn by the wind in the sand.

There seemed to be nothing that faintly resembled crops.

Orthoptera—small-winged crickets and white-whiskered earwigs.

Rhynchota—red-striped soldier bugs. He was not certain of the name, but surely it was a type of soldier bug.

Of the sheath-winged insects which he sought: white-backed billbugs and long-legged letter-droppers.

He had not been able to spot a single one of the beetle family that was his real aim. And indeed for that very reason he was anticipating the fruits of the next day's battle.

His fatigue brought faint spots of light dancing on his retina. Then, in spite of himself, he stopped walking and fixed his eyes on the surface of the darkening dunes. It was no use; anything that moved looked like a beetle.

As he had promised, the old man was waiting for him in front of the cooperative offices.

"I'm sorry for all this trouble."

"Not at all. I only hope you'll like what I found for you."

A meeting seemed to be in session in the offices. Four or five men were sitting in a circle, from which shouts of laughter rose. On the front of the entry hung a horizontal plaque with large lettering: LOVE YOUR HOME. The old man said something; abruptly the laughing stopped, and he walked out leading the others. The shell-strewn road floated vague and white in the twilight.

He was escorted to one of the cavities on the ridge of the dunes at one end of the village.

From the ridge a narrow path went down the slope to the right. After they had walked on awhile, the old man leaned over into the darkness and, clapping his hands, shouted in a loud voice: "Hey! Granny! Hey, there!"

From the depths of the darkness at their feet a lamp flickered, and there was an answer.

"Here I am! Here! There's a ladder over by the sand-bags."

Indeed, without the ladder he could not possibly have got down. He would have had to catch hold on the cliff with his bare hands. It was almost three times the height of the house top, and even with the ladder it was still not easy to manage. In the daytime, he recalled, the slope had seemed to him rather gentle, but as he looked at it now, it was close to perpendicular. The ladder was an uncertain thing of rope, and if one lost one's balance it would get hopelessly tangled up. It was quite like living in a natural stronghold.

"You needn't worry about anything. Have a good rest."

The old man turned around and went back, without going all the way to the bottom.

Sand poured down from overhead. The man had a feeling of curiosity, as if he had returned to his childhood. He wondered whether the woman was old; she had been called granny. But the person who came to meet him, holding up a lamp, was a smallish, nice sort of woman around thirty. Perhaps she was wearing powder; for someone who lived by the sea, she was amazingly white. Anyway, he was extremely grateful for her cheerful welcome, from which she could not conceal her own pleasure.

Indeed, if it had not been for the warm reception, the house itself would have been difficult to put up with at all. He would have thought they were making a fool of him and would doubtless have gone back at once. The walls were peeling, matting had been hung up in place of sliding doors, the upright supports were warped, boards had replaced all the windows, the straw mats were on the point of rotting and when one walked on them they made a noise like a wet sponge. Moreover, an offensive smell of burned, moldering sand floated over the whole place.

Well, everything depended on one's attitude. He was disarmed by the woman's manner. He told himself that this one night was a rare experience. And, if he were lucky, he might run up against some interesting insects. It was certainly an environment in which insects would gladly live.

His premonition was right. No sooner had he taken the seat offered him beside the hearth, which was sunk in the earthen floor, than all around there was the sound of what seemed to be the pitter-patter of rain. It was an army of fleas. But he was not one to be overwhelmed by such things. An insect collector is always prepared. He had dusted the inside of his clothing with DDT, and it would be wise, before he went to sleep, to daub some insecticide on the exposed parts of his body.

"I'm just fixing something to eat. If you'll just wait a few minutes more . . ." the woman said, half standing and taking the lamp. "Can you get along without the light for a moment, please?"

"Do you only have one lamp?"

"I'm sorry, yes."

She laughed, a little embarrassed. On her left cheek a dimple appeared. Apart from her eyes, she had undeniable charm, he thought. Perhaps the look in her eyes was the result of some affliction. No matter how much make-up she used, she could not conceal the inflamed corners. Before going to bed, he decided, he would without fail apply some eye medicine too.

"It doesn't make any difference, but first I would rather like a bath."

"A bath?"

"Don't you have one?"

"I'm terribly sorry, but could you put it off until the day after tomorrow?"

"The day after tomorrow? But I won't be here the day after tomorrow." In spite of himself he laughed aloud.

"Oh?"

She turned her face away with a drawn-up expression. She was disappointed, he supposed, and, of course, with country folk there is no attempt at pretense. He ran his tongue several times over his lips with a feeling of embarrassment.

"If you don't have a bath, some water that I could pour over me would do just fine. My whole body's covered with sand."

"I'm sorry, but we don't have more than a bucketful of water either. The well is pretty far away."

She looked quite abashed, and he decided to say no more. He was soon to realize, unpleasantly, the uselessness of bathing.

The woman brought in the meal: clam soup with boiled fish. Very much a shore meal, it seemed. That was all right, but as he began to eat she opened a large paper umbrella and put it over him.

"What's that thing for?" He wondered if it were some kind of custom of the region.

"Well, if I don't put this up, the sand will get in your food."

"How is that?" he said, looking up in surprise at the ceiling, where, however, there were no holes at all.

She followed his eyes to the ceiling. "The sand sifts in everywhere. Almost an inch piles up if I don't sweep it up every day."

"Is the roof faulty?"

"Yes, pretty much so. But even if the thatching was brand-new, the sand would sift in anyway. It's really terrible. It's worse than a wood borer."

"A wood borer?"

"An insect that eats holes in wood."

"That's probably a termite, isn't it?"

"No, no. It's about this big . . . with a hard skin."

"Ah. Well, it's a long-horned saw beetle then."

"A saw beetle?"

"Long whiskers and reddish, isn't it?"

"No, it's sort of bronze-colored and shaped like a grain of rice."

"I see. Then it's an iridescent beetle."

"If you let it go on, beams like these rot away to nothing, you know."

"You mean the iridescent beetle?"

"No, the sand."

"Why?"

"It gets in from everywhere. On days when the wind direction is bad, it gets up under the roof, and if I didn't sweep it away it would soon pile up so heavy that the ceiling boards wouldn't hold it."

"Hmm. Yes, I can see it wouldn't do to let the sand accumulate in the ceiling. But isn't it funny to say that it rots the beams?"

"No. They do rot."

"But sand is essentially dry, you know."

"Anyway, it rots them. If you leave sand on brand-new wooden clogs they fall apart in half a month. They're just dissolved, they say, so it must be true."

"I don't understand the reason."

"Wood rots, and the sand rots with it. I even heard that soil rich enough to grow cucumbers came out of the roof boards of a house that had been buried under the sand."

"Impossible!" he exclaimed rudely, making a wry face. He felt that his own personal concept of sand had been defiled by her ignorance. "I know a little about sand myself. Let me tell you. Sand moves around like this all year long. Its flow is its life. It absolutely never stops—anywhere. Whether in water or air, it moves about free and unrestricted. So, usually, ordinary living things are unable to endure life in it, and this goes for bacteria too. How shall I put it . . . sand represents purity, cleanliness. Maybe it serves a preservative function, but there is certainly no question of its rotting anything. And, what's more, dear lady, to begin with, sand is a respectable mineral. It couldn't possibly rot away!"

She stiffened and fell silent. Under the protection of the umbrella which she was holding, the man, as if hurried, finished eating without a word. On the surface of the umbrella so much sand had collected he could have written in it with his finger.

And the damp was unbearable. The sand of course was not damp; it was his body that was damp. Above the roof the wind moaned. He drew out his cigarettes, and his pocket was full of sand. He had the feeling he could taste the bitterness even before he lit one.

He took an insect out of the bottle of potassium cyanide. Before it stiffened he fixed it with pins; at least he could preserve the shape of the legs. From the washstand outside came the sound of the woman cleaning dishes. Did no one else live in the house? he wondered.

When she returned she silently began to prepare the bed in a corner of the room. If she put his bed here, where in heaven's name did she intend to sleep? Naturally, in that inner room beyond the hanging mat. Besides these two there didn't seem to be anything that faintly resembled a room. But it was a very strange way of doing things—to put the guest in the room by the entry and let the hostess sleep in the inner one. Or did she have an invalid unable to move sleeping in the inner room? he wondered. Maybe. Certainly it would be much more natural to assume so. In the first place, one could hardly expect a solitary woman to go to much trouble looking after passing travelers.

"Are there other people . . . ?"

"What do you mean, 'other people'?"

"People in your family or . . ."

"No, I'm quite alone." The woman seemed to be aware of his thoughts and suddenly gave a forced and awkward laugh. "Everything really gets so damp because of the sand, even the blankets."

"Well, what about your husband?"

"Oh, yes. Last year in the typhoon . . ." she said, busying herself unnecessarily with smoothing and patting down the edges of the matting which she had finished spreading out. "Typhoons are terrible around here. The sand comes thundering down like a waterfall. Ten or twenty feet pile up in a night no matter what you do."

"As much as twenty feet?"

"At times like that, you can't ever catch up with the sand no matter how much you shovel. He ran out with my little girl—she was in middle school then—yelling that the chicken houses were in danger. I was too busy taking care of the house and had to stay in. When morning finally came and the wind died down, I went out to look. There wasn't a trace of the chicken houses . . . or anything else."

"Were they buried?"

"Yes, completely."

"That was awful! Horrible! The sands are frightful."

Suddenly the lamp began to sputter.

"It's the sand."

She got down on all fours and stretched out her arm. Laughing, she snapped the lamp wick with her finger. At once it burned brightly again. In the same posture she gazed at the flame, smiling that unnatural smile. He realized that it was doubtless deliberately done to show off her dimple, and unconsciously his body stiffened. He thought it especially indecent of her just after she had been speaking of her loved ones' death.

5

~~~~~~~~~~~~~~~~~~~~~

"HEY, there! We've brought a shovel and cans for the other one!"

A clear voice, considering that it came from a distance, broke the tension; perhaps they were using a megaphone. And then came the sound of something like tin containers striking against one another as they fell. The woman rose to answer.

He had the exasperating feeling that something underhanded was going on.

"What's that? See, there's somebody else after all."

"Oh, for goodness' sake!" She twisted her body as if she had been tickled.

"But somebody just said 'for the other one.' "

"Hmm. Well, they're referring to you."

"To me? Why mention me in connection with a shovel . . . ?"

"Never mind. Don't pay any attention. Really, they're so nosy!"

"Was there some mistake?"

However, the woman didn't answer this, and swinging around on her knees, she stepped down on the earthen floor.

"Pardon me, but are you still using the lamp?"

"Well, I haven't really finished with it. Why? Do you need it out there?"

"No, this is work I'm used to."

She put on a straw hat, of the kind used for gardening, and slipped out into the darkness.

Bending his head to one side, the man lit another cigarette. There was something definitely suspicious, he felt. He arose quietly and decided to peek behind the suspended matting. There was indeed a room, but no bed. In its place the sand had swept down in a gentle curve from beyond the wall. He shuddered involuntarily and stood rooted to the spot. This house was already half dead. Its insides were half eaten away by tentacles of ceaselessly flowing sand. Sand, which didn't even have a form of its own—other than the mean 1/8-mm. diameter. Yet not a single thing could stand against this shapeless, destructive power. The very fact that it had no form was doubtless the highest manifestation of its strength, was it not?

But he returned to reality at once. Supposing this room could not be used. Where in heaven's name did she intend to sleep? He could hear her coming and going beyond the board wall. The hands of his wrist watch pointed to 8:02. What could there be to do, he wondered, at such an hour?

He stepped down to the earthen floor in search of water. A red metallic film floated on the thimbleful of liquid remaining in the bottom of the water jar. But even that was better than enduring the sand in his mouth. When he had washed his face in the water and wiped the back of his neck, he felt considerably better.

A chilly draft was blowing along the dirt floor. Probably it was more bearable outside. He squeezed through the sliding door, which, stuck in the sand, no longer moved, and went out. The breeze blowing down from the road had indeed become much cooler. The sound of what seemed to be the motor of a three-wheeled pickup truck came to him on the wind. And when he strained his ears he could hear a number of people. Moreover—was it his imagination?—he sensed greater animation than during the day. Or was it the sound of the sea? The sky was heavy with stars.

The woman turned when she saw the lamplight. Skillfully handling the shovel, she was scooping sand into a big kerosene can. Beyond her the wall of black sand soared precipitously up and seemed to be bending inward on them. It must have been up there that he had walked during the day in his search for insects. When two kerosene cans were full, the woman carried them, one in each hand, over to where he was. As she passed him she raised her eyes. "Sand," she said in a nasal voice. She emptied the sand from the kerosene cans near the path in the back where the rope ladder hung. Then she wiped away the sweat with the end of a towel. The place was already piled high with the sand she had hauled over.

"I'm clearing away the sand."

"You'll never finish, no matter how long you work at it."

The next time she passed, she poked him in the side with the end of a free finger. He almost let the lamp fall as he started up in surprise. Should he keep holding the lamp as he was, or should he put it on the ground and return the tickling? He hesitated, caught off guard by the unexpected choice he faced. He decided to keep the lamp in his hand, and with his face set in a grin, which he himself did not know the meaning of, he awkwardly and stiffly approached the woman, who had begun to shovel again. As he drew near, her shadow filled the whole surface of the sand wall.

"You shouldn't do that, you know," she said in a low, breathless voice, her back still toward him. "I have six cans to go until the lift basket comes."

His expression hardened. It was unpleasant to have feelings that he had been at pains to check aroused to no purpose. Yet, in spite of himself something not to be denied was welling up in his veins. The sand which clung to his skin was seeping into his veins and, from the inside, undermining his resistance.

"Well, shall I give you a hand?"

"Oh, that's all right. It wouldn't be right to have you do anything on the very first day."

"On the first day? Don't worry about such things. I'll only be here tonight anyway."

"Is that so?"

"I don't lead a life of leisure, you know. Hand me the other shovel. Come on."

"Excuse me, but your shovel is over there."

Indeed, under the eaves near the entrance a shovel and two kerosene cans with handles were lined up to the side. When they had said "for the other one," it was most certainly these things that had been tossed down from the road above. The preparations were too good, and he had the feeling that they had guessed in advance what he would do. But how could they? He had not known himself. Anyway, he thought apprehensively, they had a pretty low opinion of him. The shaft of the shovel was made of a bumpy wood and had a dark sheen from handling. He had already lost his desire to lend a hand.

"Oh! The lift basket is already at the neighbors'!"

She spoke animatedly, seeming not to have noticed his hesitation. Her voice was cheerful and contained a note of confidence that had not been there before. The human sounds that had been audible for some time were suddenly near at hand. A series of short, rhythmic shouts was repeated several times, followed by a period of low, continuous muttering interspersed with suppressed laughter, and then the shouts again. The rhythm of the work suddenly made him feel buoyant. In such a simple world it was probably quite normal to let a night's guest use a shovel. And there would be something curious about holding back. With his heel he made a hollow in the sand, in which he placed the lamp so that it would not fall.

"I suppose it's all right to dig any place, isn't it?"

"Well . . . not just any place."

"Then what about over here?"

"Yes, but try to dig right down from the cliff wall."

"Is this the time for clearing away the sand at all the houses?"

"Yes. The sand is easier to work with at night because it's damp. When the sand is dry," she said, looking up toward the sky, "you never know when or where it will come crashing down."

He peered up, and indeed a brow of sand, like drifted snow, bulged out from the lip of the cliff.

"But that's dangerous, isn't it?"

"It's really quite safe," she said in a laughing tone, different from her usual voice. "Look! The mist's beginning to come in."

"Mist?"

As she spoke the expanse of stars rapidly grew patchy and began to fade. A tangled filmy cloud swirled around fitfully where the wall of sand met the sky.

"You see, it's because the sand soaks up a lot of fog. When salty sand is full of fog, it gets hard like starch."

"I can't believe it!"

"Oh, yes, it's true. When the tide along the beach goes down, even big tanks can drive over the sand with no trouble."

"Amazing!"

"It's quite true. So that part that sticks out there gets bigger every night. On days when the wind comes from a bad direction, the sand comes down like today, on the umbrella. In the afternoon, when it's good and dry, it comes crashing down all at once. And it's the end if it falls in the wrong place . . . where the pillars are weak."

Her topics of conversation were restricted. Yet once she entered her own sphere she suddenly took on a new animation. This might also be the way to her heart. He was not particularly interested in what she had to say, but her words had a warmth in them that made him think of the body concealed beneath the coarse work trousers.

Then, with all his strength, he repeatedly thrust the dented cutting edge of his shovel into the sand at his feet.

6

WHEN he had finished carrying the kerosene cans over the
second time, he heard the sound of voices, and on the road
above a hand lamp flickered.

The woman spoke rather sharply.

"It's the lift basket. I've already finished over here. Give
me some help over there, will you?" For the first time he
grasped the meaning of the sandbags that lay buried at
the top of the ladder: by running the ropes around them,
the baskets could be raised and lowered. Four men managed each basket, and there were two or three groups in
all. For the most part, they appeared to be young men who
worked briskly and efficiently. By the time the basket of
one group was full, the next group was already waiting to
take over. In six hauls, the sand which had been piled up
was completely leveled off.

"Those fellows are amazing!"

His tone was friendly as he wiped away the sweat with
his shirt sleeve. The young men, who uttered not a word of
ridicule at his helping with the sand, appeared to devote
themselves energetically to their work. He felt well disposed toward them.

"Yes. In our village we really follow the motto 'Love
Your Home.'"

"What sort of love is that?"

"It's the love you have for where you live."

"Great!"

He laughed, and she laughed with him. But she did not seem to understand the reason for her laughter herself.

From afar came the sound of a three-wheeled truck starting up.

"Well now, shall we take a rest?"

"Oh, no. When they finish with one round they come right back again with the basket."

"Oh, let it go. The rest can wait until tomorrow and . . ."

He arose unconcerned and began walking toward the earthen floor, but she showed no signs of coming along with him.

"You can't do things that way! We've got to work at least once all around the house."

"What do you mean, 'all around'?"

"Well, we can't let the house be smashed, can we? The sand comes down from all sides."

"But it'll take until morning to do that."

As though challenged, she turned abruptly and hurried off. She apparently intended to return to the base of the cliff and continue her work. Quite like the behavior of the beetle, he thought.

Now that he understood this, he certainly wouldn't be taken in again.

"I'm dumfounded! Is it like this every night?"

"The sand never stops. The baskets and the three-wheeler keep going the whole night through."

"I suppose they do." And indeed they did. The sand never stopped falling. The man was completely at a loss. He was bewildered, rather as if he had casually stepped on the tail of a snake that he had thought to be small but had turned out to be surprisingly large; by the time he had realized this, its head was already threatening him from behind.

"But this means you exist only for the purpose of clearing away the sand, doesn't it?"

"Yes, but we just can't sneak away at night, you know."

He was more and more upset. He had no intention of becoming involved in such a life.

"Yes, you can. It would be simple, wouldn't it? You can do anything if you want to."

"No, that wouldn't be right at all." She spoke casually, breathing in rhythm with her shoveling. "The village keeps going because we never let up clearing away the sand like this. If we stopped, in ten days the village would be completely buried. Next it will be the neighbor's turn in back. See, there."

"Very praiseworthy, I'm sure. And do the basket gangs work so hard for the same reason?"

"Well, they do get some pay from the town."

"If they have that much money, why don't they build a more permanent hedge of trees against the sand?"

"It seems to be much cheaper to do it this way . . . when you figure the costs."

"This way? Is this really a way?" Suddenly a feeling of anger welled up in him. He was angry at the things that bound the woman . . . and at the woman who let herself be bound. "Why must you cling so to such a village? I really don't understand. This sand is not a trifling matter. You're greatly mistaken if you think you can set yourself up against it with such methods. It's preposterous! Absurd! I give up. I really give up. I have absolutely no sympathy for you."

Tossing the shovel on the kerosene cans which had been left out, he abruptly returned to the room, ignoring the expression on the woman's face.

He spent a sleepless night, turning and tossing. He pricked up his ears, sensing the woman's presence. He felt somewhat guilty. Taking such a stand in front of her was actually an expression of jealousy at what bound her; and was it not also a desire that she should put aside her work and come secretly to his bed? Actually, his strong feelings were apparently not simply anger at female stupidity. There was something more unfathomable. His mattress was getting damper and damper, and the sand more and more clammy to his skin. It was all too unreasonable, too eerie. There was no need to blame himself for having thrown the shovel aside and come in. He did not have to take that much responsibility. Besides, the obligations he had to assume were already more than enough. In fact, his involvement with sand and his insect collecting were, after all, simply ways to escape, however temporarily, from his obligations and the inactivity of his life.

No matter how he tried, he could not sleep.

The sound of the woman's movements continued without interruption. Again and again the sound of the basket drew near, and then receded. If things went on this way he would be in no condition for tomorrow's work. The next day he would get up at daybreak, he decided, and put the day to good use. The more he tried to sleep, the more wide awake he became. His eyes began to smart; his tears and his blinking seemed to be ineffective against the ceaselessly falling sand. He spread out a towel and wrapped it over his head. It was difficult to breathe, but it was better this way.

He tried thinking of something else. When he closed his eyes, a number of long lines, flowing like sighs, came floating toward him. They were ripples of sand moving over the dunes. The dunes were probably burned onto his retina because he had been gazing steadily at them for some twelve hours. The same sand currents had swallowed up and destroyed flourishing cities and great empires. They called it the "sabulation" of the Roman Empire, if he remembered rightly. And the village of something or other, which Omar Khayyám wrote of, with its tailors and butchers, its bazaars and roadways, entwined like the strands of a fish net. How many years of strife and petitioning had been necessary to change just one strand! The cities of antiquity, whose immobility no one doubted. . . . Yet, after all, they too were unable to resist the law of the flowing 1/8-mm. sands.

Sand. . . .

Things with form were empty when placed beside sand. The only certain factor was its movement; sand was the antithesis of all form. However, beyond the thin wall of boards the woman continued shoveling as usual. What in heaven's name could she hope to accomplish with her frail arms? It was like trying to build a house in the sea by brushing the water aside. You floated a ship on water in accordance with the properties of water.

With that thought he was suddenly released from the compulsive feeling of oppression that, in some strange manner, the sound of the woman's shoveling exerted on him. If a ship floated on water, then it would also float on sand. If they could get free from the concept of stationary houses, they wouldn't have to waste energy fighting the sands. A ship—a house—which flowed along, borne up by the sand . . . shapeless towns and cities.

Sand, of course, was not a liquid. There was no reason, therefore, to expect it to be buoyant. If one were to toss something on it with a lesser specific gravity, say a cork stopper, and leave it there, even the cork would sink. A boat that would float on sand would have to possess much different qualities. It could be a house shaped like a barrel, for example, which would pitch and toss. Even if it heaved over a little, it would shed whatever sand had fallen on it and rise at once to the surface. Of course, people would not be able to endure the instability of a house that kept revolving all the time. There would have to be a double-barrel arrangement on an axis, so that the bottom of the inner barrel would always have a fixed point of gravity. The inner one would remain steady; only the outer one would turn. A house which would move like the pendulum of a great clock . . . a cradle house . . . a desert ship. . . .

Villages and towns in constant movement composed of groupings of these ships. . . .

Without being aware of it, he dropped off to sleep.

7

~~~~~~~~~~~~~~~~~~~~~~~~~~~~~~~~~~~

HE was awakened by a cock's crow, like the creaking of a rusty swing. It was a restless, hangnail awakening. He had the feeling that it was barely dawn, but the hands of his wrist watch had already turned to 11:16. So the color of the sunbeams was actually that of noon. It was gloomy here because he was at the bottom of a hole and the sun had not yet reached that far.

Quickly he jumped up. The sand that had accumulated on his face, head, and chest fell away with a rustling sound. Around his nose and lips sand was encrusted, hardened by perspiration. He scraped it off with the back of his hand and cautiously blinked his eyes. Tears welled up uncontrollably under his gritty, feverish eyelids. But the tears alone were not enough to wash away the sand that had become lodged in the moist corners of his eyes.

He started toward the container on the earthen floor for a little water. Suddenly he heard the breathing of the sleeping woman on the other side of the sunken hearth and looked over. He swallowed his breath, quite forgetting the aching of his eyelids.

She was stark naked.

She seemed to float like a blurred shadow before his tear-filled eyes. She lay face up on the matting, her whole body, except her head, exposed to view; she had placed her left hand lightly over her lower abdomen, which was smooth and full. The parts that one usually covered were completely bare, while the face, which anybody would show, was concealed under a towel. No doubt the towel was to protect her nose, mouth, and eyes from the sand, but the contrast seemed to make the naked body stand out even more.

The whole surface of her body was covered with a coat of fine sand, which hid the details and brought out the feminine lines; she seemed a statue gilded with sand. Suddenly a viscid saliva rose from under his tongue. But he could not possibly swallow it. Were he to swallow, the sand that had lodged between his lips and teeth would spread through his mouth. He turned toward the earthen floor and spat. Yet no matter how much he ejected he could not get rid of the gritty taste. No matter how he emptied his mouth the sand was still there. More sand seemed to issue constantly from between his teeth.

Fortunately the water jar had recently been replenished and was brimming full. When he had rinsed his mouth and washed his face he felt better. Never before had he been so keenly aware of the marvel of water. Water was an inorganic substance like sand, a simple, transparent, inorganic substance that adapted to the body more readily than any living thing. As he let the water trickle slowly down his throat, he imagined stone-eating animals.

Again he turned and looked toward the woman. But he had no desire to go any closer. A sand-covered woman was perhaps attractive to look at but hardly to touch.

With daylight, the exasperation and excitement of the preceding night seemed pure fantasy. Of course, the whole thing would be good material for conversation. The man again looked around, as if to fix what had already become a memory, and hurriedly began to get ready. His shirt and trousers were loaded with sand. However, there was no sense worrying about such things. It was more difficult to shake all the sand from the fibers of his clothes than to get the dandruff off his head.

His shoes, too, were buried in the sand.

He wondered if he should say something to the woman before he left. But, on the other hand, it would only embarrass her to be awakened. Anyway, what should he do about paying her for the night's lodging? Perhaps it would be better to stop on the way back through the village and give the old man from the cooperative the money—the one who had brought him here the day before.

Stealthily he went out.

The sun was boiling mercury, poised at the edge of the sand cliff. Little by little it was beginning to heat the bottom of the hole. He hastily turned his eyes away from the intense glare. In the next instant he had already forgotten it. He simply stared at the façade of the sand wall.

It was unbelievable! The rope ladder had vanished from the place it had been the night before.

The marker bags, half buried by the sand, were perfectly

visible. There was no mistake, he remembered the spot. He wondered: Had the ladder alone been swallowed up by the sand? He rushed to the wall and sank his arms into the sand, groping for it. The sand gave way, unresisting, and ran down. However, he wasn't trying to find a needle in a haystack; if he did not succeed with the first try, he never would, no matter how much he searched. Stifling his rising apprehension, he looked again in blank amazement at the abruptness of the slope.

Wasn't there some spot where it could be scaled? he wondered. He circled the house two or three times, looking. If he climbed up on the roof of the house, the distance to the rim of the hole would be shortest on the north side, toward the sea, but it would still be over thirty feet. And, what was more, the wall there was steeper than anywhere else. The massive brow of sand which hung down seemed exceedingly dangerous.

The west wall seemed to be a comparatively gentle incline, having a curved surface like the inside of a cone. At an optimistic estimate it was probably around fifty or even forty-five degrees. Cautiously he took a probing step. With each step forward he slid back a half step. Even so, it looked as though he could make it with a very great effort.

Things went as he had expected for the first five or six steps. And then his feet began to sink into the sand. Before he knew whether he was making progress or not, he was buried up to his knees and seemed to have lost all power of movement. Then he attempted frantically to scramble up on all fours. The burning sand scorched his palms. Sweat poured from his whole body. Sand and sweat blinded him. Soon he had cramps in his legs and was unable to move them at all.

He stopped struggling and caught his breath, assuming he had already covered a considerable distance, but when he opened his eyes, squinting, he was amazed to find that he had come not even five yards. What exactly had he accomplished by all this effort? he wondered. Moreover, the incline he had climbed seemed to be far steeper than when he had looked at it from below. And above where he stood, it looked even worse. Although he had wanted to climb up, he seemed to have spent all his energy simply burrowing into the sand wall. The brow of sand just above his face blocked his path. In desperation he tried to struggle on a little further, but the instant he reached out for the sand over his head his footing gave way.

He was spewed out from the sand and flung to the bottom of the hole. His left shoulder made a sound like the splitting of chopsticks. But he did not notice any pain. For some time fine sand rustled gently down the face of the cliff as if to ease the hurt he had received; then it stopped. Anyway, his injury was an exceedingly small one.

It was still too soon to be frightened.

He stifled a desire to scream and slowly crept back to the hut. The woman was still sleeping in the same position. He called her, gently at first and then in a louder and louder voice. Instead of answering, she turned over as though annoyed.

The sand ran from her body, revealing her bare arms and shoulders, the nakedness of her flanks and loins. But there were more important things to think of. Going to her, he tore the towel from her head. Her face was covered with blotches, and, compared with her body, which had been encased in sand, it was gruesomely raw. The strange whiteness of her face the night before in the lamplight must surely have been produced by a powder. Now the white stuff had rubbed away, leaving bald patches that gave the impression of a cheap cutlet not cooked in batter. With surprise he realized that the white stuff was perhaps real wheat flour.

Finally she half opened her eyes, seeming to be dazzled by the light. Seizing her shoulders and shaking her, the man spoke rapidly and imploringly.

"Say, the ladder's gone! Where's the best place to climb out of here, for heaven's sake? You can't get out of a place like this without a ladder."

She gathered up the towel with a nervous gesture, and with unexpected energy slapped her face with it two or three times and then, completely turning her back to him, crouched with her knees doubled beneath her and her face to the floor. Was it a bashful movement? This was hardly the place. The man let out a shout as if a dam had given way.

"This is no joking matter! I don't know what I'll do if you don't get that ladder out. I'm in a hurry! Where in God's name did you hide it? I've had enough of your pranks. Give it here. At once!"

But she did not answer. She remained in the same position, simply shaking her head left and right.

He stiffened. His vision blurred, his breathing faltered

and almost stopped; he abruptly realized the pointlessness
of his questioning. The ladder was of rope. A rope ladder
couldn't stand up by itself. Even if he got his hands on it
there was no possibility of setting it up from below—
which meant that the woman had not taken it down, but
someone else had taken it away from the road above. His
unshaven face, smudged with sand, suddenly looked miserable.

The woman's actions and her silence took on an unexpected and terrible meaning. He refused to believe it, yet in
his heart he knew his worst fears had come true. The ladder had probably been removed with her knowledge, and
doubtless with her full consent. Unmistakably she was
an accomplice. Of course her posture had nothing to do
with embarrassment; it was the posture of a sacrificial victim, of a criminal willing to accept any punishment. He
had been lured by the beetle into a desert from which there
was no escape—like some famished mouse.

He sprang up and, hurrying to the door, looked out
again. The wind had risen. The sun was almost directly over
the hole. Heat waves, glistening as if alive, rose from the
burning sand. The sand cliff towered higher and higher
above him; its omniscient face seemed to tell his muscles
and bones the meaninglessness of resistance. The hot air
penetrated his skin. The temperature began to rise higher.

As if he had gone mad, he began to yell—he did not
know what, his words were without meaning. He simply
shouted with all the strength of his voice, as though he
could make the bad dream come to its senses, excuse itself
for its blundering, and whisk him from the bottom of the

hole. But his voice, unaccustomed to shouting, was fragile and wan. Moreover, his words were absorbed by the sand and blown by the wind, and there was no way of knowing how far they reached.

Suddenly a horrible sound interrupted him. As the woman had predicted the night before, the brow of sand on the north side had lost its moisture and collapsed. The whole house seemed to let out a soulful shriek, as if mortally wounded, and a gray blood began to drop down with a rustling sound from the new gap between the eaves and the wall. The man began to tremble, his mouth full of saliva. It was as if his own body had been crushed.

This entire nightmare could not be happening. It was too outlandish. Was it permissible to snare, exactly like a mouse or an insect, a man who had his certificate of medical insurance, someone who had paid his taxes, who was employed, and whose family records were in order? He could not believe it. Perhaps there was some mistake; it was bound to be a mistake. There was nothing to do but assume that it was a mistake.

First of all, there was no point at all in doing what they had done to him. He was not a horse or a cow; they could not force him to work against his will. Since he was useless as manpower, there was no sense in shutting him up within these walls of sand. It simply inflicted a dependent on the woman.

But somehow he was not sure. Looking at the sand wall that encircled him as if to strangle him, he was unpleasantly reminded of his miserable failure to scale it. He had simply floundered about. A feeling of impotence paralyzed his whole body. The village was already corroded by the sand, common everyday conventions were not observed; perhaps it had become a world apart. For that matter, if he wanted to be suspicious, there was plenty to be suspicious about. For example, if it was true that the kerosene cans and the shovel had been prepared especially for him, it was also true that the rope ladder had been removed without his knowing it. Furthermore, the fact that the woman had not offered a word of explanation, that she had silently accepted everything with a strange submissiveness, lent substance to the danger in the situation. The woman's remark the night before, intimating that his stay was to be a long one, had perhaps not been a mere slip of the tongue.

Then there was a small avalanche of sand.

Apprehensively, he returned to the hut. He went directly to the woman, who had remained crouching. He raised his left hand threateningly. His eyes glittered as he stood there agonizing. But halfway through the gesture, his arm, which he had raised with such purpose, suddenly collapsed. Perhaps he would feel better if he slapped the naked woman. But wouldn't this be just the part he was expected to play? She was waiting for it. Punishment inflicted, in other words, would mean that the crime had been paid for.

He turned his back on her, sank down on the ramp around the raised part of the floor, and cradled his head in his arms. Without raising his voice he began to groan. He tried to swallow the saliva that had gathered in his mouth, but it stuck in his throat and he gagged. The mucous lining of his throat had become hypersensitive to the presence of the sand; he would never get used to it no matter how long he stayed there. His saliva had become a brownish scum that oozed from the corners of his mouth. When he had finished spitting he could feel the harshness of the sand even more. He tried to dislodge it, running the tip of his tongue over the inside of his mouth and repeatedly spitting, but there was no end to it. His mouth was parched and hot, as if some inflammation had set in.

It was no use. Anyway, he would talk to the woman and try to get her to explain things more precisely. If the situation were clarified, perhaps he could decide on an attack. He could not be without a plan of action. Such a stupid situation was unbearable. But what would he do if she would not answer? That, indeed, would be the most ominous response of all. And there was ample possibility of it. Her stubborn silence! The way she seemed like a defenseless victim, crouching there with her knees drawn up under her!

The sight of her naked back was indecent and animal-like. She looked as though she could be flipped over just by bringing his hand up her crotch. No sooner had the thought crossed his mind than he caught his breath, ashamed. He had the feeling it would not be long before he would see himself as an executioner, torturing the woman, standing over her sand-spattered buttocks. Yes, eventually it would happen. And in that movement he would lose his right to speak.

Suddenly a piercing pain stuck his belly. His bladder, apparently swollen to the breaking point, cried out for relief.

8

~~~~~~~~~~~~~~~~~~~~

HE finished urinating and, stupefied with despair, remained standing as he was in the heavy air. There was no hope that things would be better as time went by. Yet he could not bring himself to go back into the house. When he left the woman's side he realized all the more how hazardous it was to be with her. No, he thought, the problem was not she herself, but that crouching position. He had never seen anything quite so indecent. It was out of the question to go back in to her. In every way that position of hers was exceedingly dangerous.

Certain types of insects and spiders, when unexpectedly attacked, fall into a paralytic state, a kind of epileptic seizure . . . an airport whose control tower has been seized by lunatics . . . a fragmented picture. He wanted to believe that his own lack of movement had stopped all movement in the world, the way a hibernating frog abolishes winter.

As his thoughts ran on, the rays of the sun had become even more intense. He made a sudden bending movement as if to protect himself from the spear thrusts of light. Abruptly lowering his head, he grasped his shirt collar and pulled with all his might. The three top buttons flew off. Scraping away the sand that clung to his palms, he remembered once again the words of the woman the night before—to the effect that the sand was never dry but always moist enough to cause the gradual disintegration of anything it touched. When he had taken off his shirt, he loosened his belt and let the air circulate inside his trousers. But it was nothing to make such a fuss about. The unpleasant feeling left him as quickly as it had come. The moisture in the sand evidently lost its magical powers as soon as it came into contact with air.

At that instant it came to him that he had made a serious mistake. His interpretation of the woman's nakedness would seem to be too arbitrary. Though he could not rule out some secret wish on her part to seduce him, perhaps this nakedness was a very ordinary habit, made necessary by the life she led. After all, she did go to bed when it got light. Anyone is apt to perspire while asleep. Her nakedness was perfectly normal seeing that she had to sleep during the day and, what was more, in a bowl of burning sand. If he were in her position, he would certainly choose to be naked too if he could.

This realization suddenly eased his feelings of tension, as if the fluttering breeze had visibly separated the sweat from the sand on his skin. There was no use stirring up groundless fears. Men have escaped through any number of concrete walls and iron bars. He would not quail simply at the sight of a padlock without finding out whether it was locked or not. He went slowly back in the direction of the hut, dragging his feet in the sand. This time he would be composed, and he would get the necessary information out of her. By getting himself in such a state and screaming at her, he could only expect her to clam up. Besides, her silence was probably only shame at having been careless enough to be caught sleeping naked.

9

To his eyes, recently exposed to the burning sand, the interior of the hut lay in semi-darkness and felt cool and damp. The hot air had a stuffy, musty smell, quite different from the outside. But suddenly he was aware of what had to be a hallucination.

The woman was not there. For a moment he was startled. He had had enough of guessing games. But there was no riddle to be solved. She *was* there. She stood looking down, her back toward him, in front of the water jar by the sink.

She had finished dressing. He had no fault to find with her. The color of her matching bluish-green kimono and work trousers gave him a sense of mintlike freshness. Indeed, he was worrying too much. Between lack of sleep and the strange environment, he could scarcely help but have wild fancies.

The woman put one hand on the rim of the water jar and peered into it; with the tip of a finger she slowly stirred the surface of the water round and round. He vigorously swung his shirt in the air—it was heavy with the dampness of sweat and sand—and wound it firmly around his wrist.

She looked around apprehensively, and her features tensed. Her solicitous manner was so natural that one would have thought she had spent her whole life with such an expression on her face. He decided to behave as casually as possible.

"Hot, isn't it? Heavens, you can't wear a shirt when it's this hot!"

Yet she still appeared suspicious and looked dolefully at him. She gave a timid and artificial laugh, and spoke hesitantly.

"Yes, it really is. You'll get a sand rash right away if you leave your clothes on when you perspire."

"A sand rash?"

"Yes. The skin festers, like after a burn, and then scales off."

"Hmm. I wonder if it really scales. It molders, I should say, with the humidity."

"Yes. . . . That's why. . . ." Maybe she was beginning to relax at last, her tongue was loosening. "When we're likely to perspire, that's why we go around with no clothes as much as we can. After all, we live down in these holes, so we don't really have to worry about anybody seeing us."

"Of course. Look, I don't want to put you to any trouble, but I would like to get this shirt washed."

"Certainly, I'll be glad to. They'll be bringing our drum of water tomorrow."

"Tomorrow? Tomorrow will be a problem," he chuckled. Actually he had cleverly maneuvered the conversation to his subject. "Incidentally, when in heaven's name are they going to let me out of here? I'm going to be in a real fix. If a salaried worker like me breaks his schedule even by a half day, he stands to lose a lot. I don't want to waste a minute. There are a lot of coleoptera hopping around in sandy soil like this. I wonder if you know of any. I wanted to find a new species on this vacation."

She moved her lips faintly. But no words came out. Perhaps she was just repeating the unaccustomed name. He realized that her mind was again closing. He went on instinctively.

"Say, I wonder if there isn't some way of getting in touch with the villagers, like beating on a kerosene can or something."

But she made no answer. She again fell into her passive silence as quickly as a stone sinks into water.

"What's the matter with you? Damn it! Why don't you say anything?" Again his nerves were on edge, but he somehow stifled his desire to shout. "I don't get it. If there's some misunderstanding, all right! There's no use crying over spilt milk. This silence of yours is the worst thing. My pupils are always doing that, but I tell them that the most cowardly thing they can do is to clam up and pretend to take the blame themselves. If there's any explanation, out with it at once."

"But . . ." Her eyes wavered toward her elbow, but in a surprisingly firm voice she said: "I think you already understand."

"I understand . . . ?" He gasped, unable to conceal his shock.

"Yes, you must have understood by now."

"But, I don't understand!" he finally shouted. "How should I understand? You can't expect me to understand when you never say a word, can you?"

"Well, life here is really too hard for a woman alone."

"What's that got to do with me?"

"It does have something to do with you. I'm afraid I've acted wrong toward you."

"What do you mean, 'acted wrong'?" he said, stumbling over his words in his eagerness. "In other words, why the conspiracy? You baited the trap. You thought I'd spring at once if a woman was there, like some dog or cat."

"It's getting to be the season now when the winds come from the north and we worry about the sand storms," she said, glancing at the wooden door, which was standing open. There was a foolish confidence in her quiet, monotonous voice.

"It's no joke! There's a limit to absurdity. This is illegal detention pure and simple. A fine crime! You don't have to do such senseless things. Any number of men out of work would be glad of the chance for daily pay."

"Maybe. But it would make trouble if they knew outside about things here."

"And do you people think you're safe with me? Indeed you're not! You've made a real mistake if you think you are. I'm no tramp—unfortunately for you. I pay my taxes, and I'm a registered resident. There'll soon be a request out for an investigation, and then you'll see. Don't you people even understand that? Just how do you expect to justify yourselves? Now, go and call whoever's responsible. I'll tell him exactly what I think about this whole stupid situation."

She lowered her eyes and sighed faintly. Her shoulders drooped, but she made no further attempt to move; she was like a dejected, unjustly abused puppy. Yet her attitude made him even more angry.

"What are you hesitating for? Come on, I'm not the only one concerned. You're as much the victim as I am, aren't you? Well, aren't you? You said yourself that if they knew on the outside about life here, there'd be trouble. That shows you yourself recognize how unreasonable this life of yours is. Stop being a mouthpiece; stop being treated like a slave. Nobody has the right to keep you shut up here. Go on and call somebody now. We're going to get out of here. . . . Ah, so that's it. You're afraid, aren't you? But that's foolish! What's there to be afraid of? I'm here. And I've got friends who work for a newspaper. We'll give the story a social angle. What's wrong? Why don't you say something? I tell you there's nothing to be afraid of!"

After a moment the woman suddenly spoke, as if to console him.

"Shall I start fixing dinner?"

10

~~~~~~~~~~~~~~~~~~~~~~

Out of the corner of his eye, he followed her figure as she began silently to peel some potatoes. Should he docilely accept the food she was preparing or not? His thoughts were completely taken up by the problem.

Now was the time to be calm and cool. Since her intentions were clear, it would be better to face the facts instead of shilly-shallying—better to lay some concrete plans for escape. He could call them to account for their unlawful treatment later. But his empty stomach weakened his will. He could not concentrate his faculties. But if he didn't want to recognize, officially, the predicament he was in, then he should probably refuse all food too. It would be ludicrous to eat the meal when he disapproved. Even a bristling dog will drop its tail as soon as it gets a bone.

But best not jump to conclusions. As long as he did not know just how far the woman would go, there was no need to be so passive. It was not a question of her doing something for nothing. He would certainly pay for his food. If he paid his money there would be no reason to feel indebted to her—not a bit. The announcers of boxing matches on television were always saying that attack was the best defense.

With this inspiration, he was relieved to have found a

good excuse for not refusing the food. Suddenly his mind cleared and he saw everything. Only the sand was his enemy. Yes, that was it. There was no particular need to pose unreasonable problems, to be broken through like iron bars. They had taken away the rope ladder—very well, he would make a ladder of wood. If the sand wall were too steep, then he would make the incline more gentle by scraping away the sand. If he would only use his head a little, it would all be easy. The plan seemed overly simple, but as long as it fitted his purpose, the simpler it was the better. The best solution—take Columbus and his egg—is often ridiculously simple. If he did not mind the trouble, if he really would fight, well, the game was not over yet.

The woman had finished peeling the potatoes; she diced them and put them into a big iron pot over the hearth, along with a large sliced radish, leaves and all. She carefully took a match out of a plastic bag, and after using it she wrapped up the bag tightly again and fastened it with a rubber band. She put rice in a sieve and poured water over it, probably to wash away the sand. The pot began to make a bubbling sound, and the pungent smell of radish hung in the air.

"There's some water left over. Would you like to wash your face?"

"No, I'd rather drink it than wash my face in it."

"Oh, I'm sorry, but I keep the drinking water separate." From under the sink she took a large kettle which was swathed in plastic. "It's not very cold, but it's been boiled, so you don't have to be afraid. . . ."

"By the way, if you don't leave a little water in the jar,

you'll be up against it when it comes to washing up later, won't you?"

"Oh, no. I clean off the dishes just by rubbing them with sand."

As she said this, she grabbed a handful of sand by the window and threw it into a plate she was holding. She swirled the sand around and covered the plate, to demonstrate the actual process. He wasn't sure whether the plate was really clean or not, but he had the feeling it probably was. The sand in this operation, at least, conformed very well with the idea he had had of it all along.

Again the meal was served under the umbrella. Lightly broiled fish and the cooked vegetables. Everything was slightly gritty with sand. They could eat together, he thought, if she would hang the umbrella from the ceiling, but he didn't want to make an express suggestion. The coarse, common tea was dark enough in color, but it had little taste.

When he had finished eating, the woman returned to the sink and, putting a piece of plastic over her head, quietly began to eat her own meal under it. She looked like some kind of insect, he thought. Did she intend to go on living like this forever? From the outside, this place seemed only a tiny spot of earth, but when you were at the bottom of the hole you could see nothing but limitless sand and sky. A monotonous existence enclosed in an eye. She had probably spent her whole life down here, without even the memory of a comforting word from anyone. Perhaps her heart was throbbing now like a girl's because they had trapped him and given him to her. It was too pitiful!

He was tempted to say something to her; for the time being, however, he decided to have a smoke, and he lit a cigarette. It would certainly appear that plastic was a necessity of life here. He got the match to light, but the cigarette had become unsmokable. He took strong drags on it, sucking in his cheeks between his teeth. Yet no matter how he puffed he got only the taste of smoke, an extremely greasy smoke that irritated his tongue; the cigarette was worse than useless. The experience quite spoiled his frame of mind and took away any desire he might have had to speak to the woman.

She attended to the dirty dishes, placing them on the earthen floor and slowly heaping up sand on them. Then she said hesitantly: "I'm going to have to begin right away getting the sand down from the ceiling."

"Getting the sand down? Oh. Well, that's all right with me." He wondered indifferently why that should have anything to do with him now. It didn't concern him if the beams rotted and the roof fell in.

"If I'm in your way, do you want me to move somewhere else?"

"I'm sorry, but would you mind . . . ?"

She needn't pretend! Why didn't she show even a little of her real feelings? In her heart she probably felt as if she had bitten into a spoiled onion. But she was expressionless as she swiftly, with an accustomed movement, wrapped a towel folded in two around the lower part of her face and tied it behind her head. She put a whisk broom and a small piece of wood under her arm, and climbed up on the partition of the closet, which had only half a door remaining.

Abruptly, he exclaimed: "Frankly, I'm convinced we'd both feel much better if this house fell to pieces!"

He was surprised himself at his peevish outburst, and the woman turned and looked at him with an even more startled look. Well, apparently she had not yet turned quite into an insect.

On he went: "No, I'm not particularly angry at *you*. It's the whole business. I don't like this scheming where you people think you can put a man in chains. Do you realize what I'm talking about? No, it doesn't make any difference whether you do or not. I'll tell you an amusing story. I used to keep a worthless mongrel at my boardinghouse. He had a terribly thick coat that scarcely shed even in summer. He was such a sorry sight that I finally decided to cut his hair. But just as I was about to throw away the hair that had been cut off, the dog—I wonder what could have been going on in his mind?—suddenly let out a pitiful howl, took a bunch of hair in his mouth, and ran into his house. He probably felt that the hair was a part of his own body and he didn't want to be separated from it." He furtively observed the woman's expression. However, she made no attempt to move, remaining bent over in an unnatural position on top of the partition. "Well, let it go. Everyone has his own philosophy that doesn't hold good for anybody else. Go on working your fingers to the bone with your sand sweeping or whatever else you will. But I can't stand it. I've had enough! I could get out of here easily if I wanted to. And I've just run out of cigarettes."

"Oh. . . . I wanted to say . . . about the cigarettes
. . . ," she said, awkwardly and submissively, "when they
deliver the water, later. . . ."

"Cigarettes? Do they bring you cigarettes too?" He
laughed in spite of himself. "That's not the question. I'm
talking about the tufts of hair. Tufts of hair. Don't you understand? What I'm trying to say is that there's no sense in
such futile concern over a tuft of hair."

She was silent. She showed no sign of offering any explanation. She waited a moment, and when it was evident
he had stopped speaking, she slowly turned as if nothing
had happened and resumed her unfinished work. She slid
back the cover over the top of the closet and crawled up,
working the upper part of her body into the aperture with
her elbows and wiggling her legs clumsily. The sand began
to fall in thin rivulets here and there. He had the feeling
that there was some strange insect inside the ceiling. Sand
and rotted wood. No, thank you, he had had enough of
strange things!

Then from one corner of the ceiling the sand began to
pour out dizzily in numerous tapelike streams. The strange
quietness was in eerie contrast to the violence of the flow
of sand. The holes and cracks in the ceiling boards were
quickly raised in exact relief on the straw matting. The
sand burned in his nose and irritated his eyes. He fled out
of the house.

Suddenly he felt as though he were melting away from
his feet upward into a landscape of flame. But something

like a perpetual shaft of ice remained in the center of his body. He felt ashamed in some way. An animal-like woman . . . thinking only in terms of today . . . no yesterday, no tomorrow . . . with a dot for a heart. A world where people were convinced that men could be erased like chalk marks from a blackboard. In his wildest dreams he could not have imagined that such barbarism still existed anywhere in the world. Well, anyway . . . if this was a sign that he was beginning to regain his composure and recover from his initial shock, his qualms of conscience were not a bad thing.

But he must not waste time. If possible, he would like to finish before it got dark. Squinting, he measured the height of the sand wall quivering behind a film of heat waves like molten glass. Every time he looked at it, it seemed to grow higher. It would be hard to go against nature and try to make a gentle slope abrupt—he only wanted to try to make a steep one more gentle. There was no reason to hang back.

The best way to do it, of course, would be to shave it down gradually from the top. Since this was impossible, he had no choice but to dig from the bottom. First he would scoop out a suitable amount of sand from below and wait for the sand above to cave in, then he would scoop more out and again let the top fall in. If he repeated this again and again, the ground level he stood on would gradually rise and ultimately reach the top. Of course, he might also be carried away by the flowing sand in the midst of the operation. But no matter how much sand flowed, it still wasn't water, and he had never yet heard about anyone being drowned in sand.

The shovel was standing with the kerosene cans against the outside wall that went around the earthen floor. The dented edge of the shovel gleamed white like a piece of cracked porcelain.

For some time he concentrated on digging. The sand was exceedingly tractable, and his work appeared to be progressing. The sound of the shovel as it bit into the sand, and his own breathing, ticked away the time. However, at last his arms began to grow weary. He thought he had worked for a considerable time, but his digging had apparently had no results at all. Only a little bit of sand had fallen from right above where he was digging. Somehow, it was working out very differently from the simple geometric process he had evolved in his head.

Rather than worry further, he decided to take advantage of a rest period and put his theory to the test by constructing a model of the hole. Fortunately, materials were plentiful. He chose a spot in the shade of the eaves and dug a hollow about a half yard wide. But the incline of the slope did not make the angle he had anticipated; it was only forty-five degrees at the most, about like a wide-mouthed mixing bowl. When he tried scooping sand from the bottom, the sand flowed down the sides, but the incline remained the same. There would appear to be a fixed angle for sand. The weight and resistance of the grains seemed to be in perfect balance. Supposing this were true, did the wall he was trying to overcome have about the same degree of incline?

No, that could not be. It might be an illusion, but it could not be true. When you looked at any incline from below it obviously appeared less than it actually was.

Then, shouldn't he perhaps consider it to be a question of quantity? The pressure would naturally change with different amounts of sand. If the pressure changed, a variation in the balance of weight and resistance would naturally occur. Perhaps it depended on the nature of the sand grains. Clay that has been packed down and clay from a natural deposit have completely different resistance to pressure. Furthermore, he had to consider the question of moisture. In short, another law was probably functioning, different from the one that applied to the model he had made.

Despite his failure, the experiment was not completely in vain. The very fact that he now realized that the slope of the wall was in what he might call a superstable state was an important find. Generally it is not particularly difficult to make a superstable state into a normally stable one.

A supersaturated solution, just by being shaken, at once produces a crystalline precipitate and moves toward the normal saturation point.

Suddenly he had the feeling that someone was near; he turned around. He had been unaware of the woman, who was standing in the doorway staring fixedly at him. He was understandably embarrassed and took a step back in confusion, glancing around as if in search of help. He raised his eyes, and there at the top of the east bank were three men, all in a row, looking down at him. They wore towels wrapped around their heads; as they were not visible from the mouth down, he could not be sure, but they seemed to be the old men of the day before. At once he straightened up, but just as suddenly he changed his mind and decided to ignore them and go on with his work. The fact that he was being watched spurred him on.

The perspiration ran into his eyes and dripped from the end of his nose. Since there was no time to wipe it away, he just closed his eyes and shoveled. Under no condition must he rest his arms. When they saw his unflagging pace, they would realize, unless they were dim-wits, how despicable they were.

He looked at his watch. He wiped it against his pants to remove the sand on its face; it was only 2:10. The same ten minutes after two as when he had looked before. He suddenly lost confidence in his pace. From a snail's point of view the sun probably moves with the speed of a baseball. He changed his grip on the shovel, and turning back again to the wall, he set frantically to work.

Suddenly the flow of sand grew violent. There was a muffled sound and then a pressure against his chest. He tried to look up to see what was happening, but he no longer had any sense of direction. He was only dimly aware of a faint milky light playing over him as he lay doubled up in the black splotch of his vomit.

PART II

~~~~~~~~~~~~~~~~~~~~~~~~~~~~~~~~

11

> *"Jabu, jabu, jabu, jabu*
> *What sound is that?*
> *It's the sound of the bell.*
>
> *"Jabu, jabu, jabu, jabu*
> *What voice is that?*
> *It's the voice of the devil."*

THE woman sang as if murmuring to herself, tirelessly repeating the same verses as she scooped the slime from the water jar.

When the song stopped, the sound of rice being ground came to his ears. He sighed gently, rolled over, and waited, his body tight with expectancy. Soon the woman brought a washbasin filled with water, probably to sponge off his body. His skin, which was puffy from sand and perspiration, was becoming inflamed. He lay there anticipating the cool, damp towel.

He had been in bed ever since he had fainted in the sand. For the first two days he had had a fever of around a hundred and had vomited constantly. But on the following day the fever had dropped and he had partially recovered his appetite. The basic cause was probably not the injury he had received in the sand avalanche, but the unaccustomed exertion he had kept up for so long, exposed to the direct rays of the sun. Anyway, in the long run, it hadn't amounted to much.

That was probably why he recovered so quickly. On the fourth day the pain in his legs and loins had almost gone away. On the fifth, except for a certain heaviness, no more symptoms were apparent. Nevertheless, he stayed in bed, giving an outward show of being seriously ill; but of course there was motive and calculation in this. Naturally, he had not for a moment abandoned his plans for escape.

"Are you awake?"

She was calling to him timidly. Out of the corner of his half-closed eyes he noticed the roundness of her knee through her work trousers. He answered her with a wordless groan. Slowly squeezing out the towel in the dented brass washbasin, she asked: "How do you feel?"

"Well . . . a little better. . . ."

"Do you want me to wipe your back?"

He did not particularly mind abandoning himself to the woman's hands since he had the excuse of being sick. He remembered vaguely that he had read a poem about a feverish child who had dreamt he was enveloped in cool, silver paper. His sand-clogged skin was suddenly cool and

fresh again. The odor of the woman slipped over his quickened body, subtly stimulating him.

Even so, he could not completely forgive her. This feeling for her was one thing, but what she had done was another, and he had to distinguish between them, at least for the time being. His three-day holiday had already gone by. It was no use struggling any more. The failure of his first plan to level off the sand slope by breaking down the cliff was due to lack of preparation as much as anything. It would have worked well if not for the sunstroke. But the labor of digging out the sand had been more exhausting than he had imagined. He had to adopt a more workable method, and thus he had hit upon this feigned illness.

When he had recovered his senses, he had been somewhat displeased to realize that he had been put to bed in the woman's house. The villagers apparently had no intention of showing him any sympathy. He understood this, but he had his own idea. They had underestimated his condition and had not called a doctor. He would make them really sorry. He would sleep soundly during the night while the woman was working, and conversely, during the day, when she had to rest, he would disturb her sleep by exaggerated complaints of pain.

"Does it hurt?"

"Of course it hurts. My spine must be dislocated some place."

"Shall I massage it?"

"My God, no! I couldn't stand being fumbled with by an amateur. Spinal nerves are vital. What would you do if I died? You'd be the ones in trouble, wouldn't you? Call a doctor. A doctor! Oh, it hurts. I can't stand this pain. If you don't hurry it'll be too late!"

The woman, unable to endure the strain of the situation, would soon be exhausted. Her capacity for work would drop, and even the safety of the building would be threatened. It would be a matter of no little importance for the village too. Far from having someone to help them work, they had got themselves a real stumbling block. If they did not get him out at once, the situation would get completely out of hand.

But this scheme too did not go as smoothly as he had anticipated. Here the nights were busier than the days . . . the sounds of the shovel which he could hear through the walls . . . the woman's breathing . . . the whistling and the cries of the men carrying the hoist baskets . . . the muffled roar of the three-wheeled truck, muted by the wind . . . the distant howling of dogs. The more he tried to sleep, the more nervous he became, and he would awaken completely.

When he did not get enough sleep at night, he could not avoid napping during the day. But what was worse was knowing that, if this idea failed, there would always be some other way of escape; and he was somewhat impatient with the present situation. It had already been a week. It would be just about now that a request for investigation would be submitted. The first three days had been his regular vacation. But after that he would be absent without notice. His colleagues, who were usually very sensitive to what other people were about, would surely not let this go unheeded. Perhaps that very evening some busybody

would appear and snoop around his boardinghouse. The
plain room, smelly and close in the afternoon sun, would
betray the absence of its owner. Perhaps the caller would
be instinctively jealous of the lucky man who had been
freed from this hole. The next day, malicious gossip would
be whispered around to the accompaniment of frowns and
raised eyebrows. That would be natural. Even he himself
could not expect this eccentric vacation to have any other
effect on his colleagues. Rarely will you meet anyone so
jealous as a teacher. Year after year students tumble along
like the waters of a river. They flow away, and only the
teacher is left behind, like some deeply buried rock at the
bottom of the current. Although he may tell others of his
hopes, he doesn't dream of them himself. He thinks of
himself as worthless and either falls into masochistic loneliness or, failing that, ultimately becomes suspicious and
pious, forever denouncing the eccentricities of others. He
longs so much for freedom and action that he can only
hate people. Was his disappearance accidental? No. If it
had been an accident, there would have been some sort of
news about him. Well, then, suicide? But that would have
involved the police. And suicide would be impossible!
Don't overrate the foolish boy. Yes, indeed, he disappeared by his own choice; there's no need to root around
any more. But it'll soon be almost a week. He really is a
scaremonger. I really don't know what he can be thinking
of.

It was doubtful whether they were sincerely worried, but
at least their meddling curiosity was as overripe as an un-
picked persimmon. Consequently, the next step would be

for the headmaster to visit the police and inquire about forms for requesting an investigation. Behind his serious face he would completely dissimulate the pleasure that was welling up within him. "*Full name*: Niki Jumpei. *Age*: thirty-one. *Height*: five feet five inches. *Weight*: a hundred and forty pounds. *Hair*: slightly thin, worn straight back; no hair oil. *Eyesight*: right 20/30; left, 20/20. *Color of skin*: darkish. *Features*: long face, a slight cast to the eyes, snub nose, square jaws; no other special characteristics except for a conspicuous mole under the left ear. *Blood type*: AB. Speaks thickly with a stammer. Introverted, stubborn, but not especially inept socially. *Clothing*: perhaps dressed for entomological work. The full-face photograph attached above was taken two months ago."

Of course even the villagers must naturally have some countermeasure in mind, for they had dared involve themselves in such a mad venture. It would be easy to fool a couple of country policemen. They must have taken some precautions to prevent them from coming around on trifling matters. But this kind of smoke screen was necessary and effective only so long as he was healthy and able to stand the work of shoveling sand. It was not worth the risk of hiding a seriously sick person who had been laid up a week as he had. If they decided he was useless, it would be advisable for them to dispose of him at once before it became too troublesome. At this point, they could cook up a story. They might say that he had been seized by strange hallucinations caused by the shock of having fallen by himself into the hole, and this explanation would be far more acceptable than his own fantastic complaints that he had been trapped and imprisoned.

Somewhere a cock crowed and a bull lowed shrilly. But in the sand hollow there was neither distance nor direction. The ordinary normal world was outside, where children played, kicking stones along the roadside, and where roosters proclaimed the end of night at the proper time. The colors of dawn were beginning to mingle with the fragrance of cooking rice.

And the woman was ardently scrubbing him. After a rough wiping with a wet towel, she scoured him as if she were polishing window glass, twisting the towel tightly until it was like a piece of wood. In addition to the sounds of morning, the rhythmical sensation of the rubbing brought him little by little to an irresistible drowsiness.

"By the way . . ." He stifled a yawn which seemed to be forcibly wrenched from within him. "It's been such a long time. . . . I would like to see a newspaper. What do you think . . . ? Do you suppose there would be any way of getting one?"

"Well . . . I'll ask . . . later."

He realized very well that she was trying to show she was sincere. He was distinctly sensitive to her concern lest she hurt his feelings, which showed in the diffident tone of her voice. But it also irritated him profoundly. Would she really ask? Didn't he have the right to read a newspaper if he liked? He pushed her hands away, railing against her, carried away by an impulse to upset the washbasin and its contents.

But getting angry at this point would spoil things. A

seriously ill person would hardly get so excited over a news-paper. Of course, he did want to see a paper. If there was no scenery to look at, it was only natural to want to see pic-tures of scenery at least. He had read in various books how landscape painting had developed in naturally spare country and how newspapers had come out of industrial areas where human relations were anonymous. Moreover, he might have the luck to find announcements of missing people; or, better yet, an article on his own disappearance might even grace a corner of the social columns. Of course, the villagers could not be expected to pass him willingly a newspaper which carried an article like that. In any case, patience was the most important thing now.

Certainly, pretending to be ill was no fun. It was like holding a taut spring enclosed in your hand. You couldn't stand it indefinitely. He could not let things go on as they were. He must really make them realize how responsible they were for him. He would see to it, starting this very day, that one way or another the woman would not get a wink of sleep!

(Don't sleep . . . ! You mustn't go to sleep!)

He stretched and gave a long, drawn-out groan.

12

~~~~~~~~~~~~~~~~~~~~~~~~

UNDER the umbrella that the woman had set up for him he sipped a tongue-burning soup containing bits of seaweed. A precipitate of sand remained in the bottom of the cup.

His memory had completely stopped functioning. Then it had gotten confused with a long, oppressive dream. In the dream he was astride an old, used chopstick, floating down some unknown street. It was not bad on the chopstick, rather like riding a scooter, but when he relaxed his attention he suddenly lost his buoyancy. The street was a dull red near at hand, and in the distance a hazy green. Something in the combination of colors disturbed him. At last he arrived at a long wooden building that looked like a barracks. The smell of cheap soap floated in the air. He mounted the stairs, hitching up his trousers, which seemed about to slip off, and came to an empty room containing only a long, narrow table. About ten men and women were seated around the table enthusiastically playing some game. The player in the center was dealing cards from a deck. At the end of the deal, the dealer suddenly gave *him* the last card and cried out. He took the card involuntarily and looked at it; it was not a card at all, but a letter. The letter had a strange, soft feel to it. When he exerted pressure with his fingers, blood came spurting up. He screamed out and awoke.

His vision was obscured by a dingy, mistlike film. There was a crackling noise of dry paper as he moved his body. His face was covered with an open newspaper. Damn! He had fallen asleep again. A film of sand fell from the surface of the paper when he brushed it aside. From the quantity of sand it would seem that quite some time had gone by. The slant of the sun's rays piercing through the cracks in the wall told him it was about noon. But what was that smell? he wondered. New ink? Impossible, he thought, yet he glanced at the date line. Wednesday, the sixteenth. It really was today's paper! It was unbelievable, but it was true. Then the woman must have passed along his request.

He propped himself up with an elbow on the mattress, which had become sodden and sticky with perspiration. All kinds of thoughts at once began to whirl around in his mind, and he tried in vain to follow the print on the long-awaited paper.

Increased Agenda for the Joint Japan-America Committee?

How in heaven's name had the woman managed to get her hands on this paper? Could it be true that the villagers were beginning to feel they owed him something? Even so, judging from how things had gone till now, all contact with the outside ceased after breakfast. Did the woman have some special way of communicating with the outside that he did not yet know of? Or, failing that, did she herself get out and buy the paper? It must certainly be one or the other.

Drastic Measures Against Traffic Jams

But just a minute. Supposing the woman had gone out—
it was inconceivable that she could have done it without
the rope ladder. He didn't know how she had managed it,
but one thing was certain—a rope ladder had been used.
A prisoner dreaming of escape was one thing, but how
could the woman, a resident of the village, put up with
losing her freedom of movement? The removal of the rope
ladder must be a temporary measure to keep him imprisoned. If that were so, and if he could keep them off guard,
someday the same opportunity would occur again.

*Ingredient in Onions Found Effective in Treatment of
Radiation Injuries*

His strategy of pretended illness seemed to have produced an unexpected return. Everything comes in time to
him who waits—they put it well in the old days. But somehow he did not react to the idea. Something in him was
still unsatisfied. Perhaps it was the fault of that weird,
terribly upsetting dream. He felt strangely uneasy about
the dangerous letter. But was it dangerous? Whatever
could it mean?

However, there was no use worrying every time he
dreamt something. In any event, he had to carry through
what he had begun.

The woman was asleep beside the sill of the raised portion of the floor around the hearth. She was breathing
gently and lay curled in a ball, holding her knees as she
always did; she had thrown an unironed summer kimono
over herself. After that first day she had stopped appear-

ing naked before him, but under the summer kimono she
was probably as bare as ever.

He glanced quickly at the society page and the local
columns. Of course, there was no article on his disappearance, no missing-person notice. But he had expected as
much and so was not particularly discouraged. He quietly
arose and stepped down on the earthen floor. He was wearing only baggy, half-length drawers made of synthetic silk,
and the upper half of his body was completely bare. It
was definitely the most comfortable way to be. Sand had
accumulated around his waist where he had tied the
drawstring and the skin there was inflamed and itchy.

He stood in the doorway and looked up at the walls of
sand. The light thrust into his eyes, and the surroundings
began to burn yellow. There was not a sign of man or rope
ladder: that seemed natural. He checked, nonetheless, just
to make sure. There was not even a sign that the rope ladder had been let down. Of course, with a wind like this, it
wouldn't have taken five minutes for any trace to disap-
pear. Just outside the doorway the surface of the sand was
continually being turned under as though there were some
current.

He came back in and lay down. A fly was flitting about.
It was a tiny light-pink fruit fly. Perhaps something was
spoiling somewhere. After he had moistened his throat
with water in the plastic-wrapped kettle by his pillow, he
addressed the woman: "Would you mind getting up a minute?"

She jumped up trembling, letting the summer kimono

fall open to her waist. The veins stood out blue in the sagging, but still full, breasts. Flustered, she adjusted her kimono. There was a vague look in her eyes, and she did not seem fully awake yet. He hesitated. Should he question her now about the ladder? Should he raise his voice in anger? Or should he adopt a mild, inquiring tone, at the same time thanking her for the newspaper? If his goal were simply to prevent her from sleeping, then it would be best to go at it rather aggressively. He had missed the mark with his feigned illness, for his behavior was scarcely that of a man who had dislocated his spine. What he had to do was make them recognize that he was no longer of any use for work—at all events, get them to relax their vigilance. They had softened to the extent of giving him a newspaper; he had to break down their resistance even more.

But he was summarily disappointed in his expectations.

"No, of course I don't go out. The men from the farm co-op happened to deliver some wood preservative I ordered a while back, and I had a chance to ask them. Only about four or five houses take newspapers in the village. They had to go all the way to the store in town to buy it."

It was not impossible that things had happened so. It was rather like being shut up in a cell with a lock that had no key. If even the people of the region themselves had to put up with imprisonment, then the precipitous wall of sand was no laughing matter for him. He became desperate and insistent.

"This is amazing! This is your house, isn't it? You're

not a dog. It should be nothing for you to come and go freely, should it? Or have you done something so bad you don't dare show your face to the villagers?"

Her eyes opened wide in surprise. The glare was so strong that they were bloodshot and red.

"Certainly not! It's nonsense to think I don't dare show my face!"

"Well, there's no reason for you to be so timid."

"But there isn't any reason to go out!"

"You can at least take a walk."

"A walk?"

"Yes. A walk. Wouldn't it be enough just to walk around a little? I mean, you used to take walks when you wanted to, before I came, didn't you?"

"Yes, but I get all tired out, walking for no particular reason."

"I'm not joking. Ask yourself. You ought to understand. Even a dog'll go mad if you keep it shut up in a cage."

"But I have taken walks," she said abruptly in her monotonous, withdrawn voice. "Really, they used to make me walk a lot. Until I came here. I used to carry a baby around for a long time. I was really tired out with all the walking."

The man was taken by surprise. Indeed, what a strange way of speaking! He was unable to answer when she turned on him like that.

Yes, he remembered, when everything was in ruins some ten years ago, everybody desperately wanted not to have to walk. And now, were they glutted with this freedom from walking? he wondered. And yet, even the child who wanted so desperately to go picnicking cried when it got lost.

The woman suddenly changed her tone and said: "Do you feel all right?"

Stop looking so stupid! He was angry; he wanted to make her admit her guilt even if he had to force it out of her. At the very thought his hair bristled and his skin felt scratchy like dry paper. "Skin" seemed to establish an association of ideas with the word "force." Suddenly she became a silhouette cut out from its background. A man of twenty is sexually aroused by a thought. A man of forty is sexually aroused on the surface of his skin. But for a man of thirty a woman who is only a silhouette is the most dangerous. He could embrace it as easily as embracing himself, couldn't he? But behind her there were a million eyes. She was only a puppet controlled by threads of vision. If he were to embrace her, he would be the next to be controlled. The big lie that he had dislocated his spine would at once be revealed in its true light. He could not stand to have his life stop even in a place like this.

The woman sidled up to him. Her knees pressed against his hips. A stagnant smell of sun-heated water, coming from her mouth, nose, ears, armpits, her whole body, began to pervade the room around him. Slowly, hesitantly, she began to run her searing fingers up and down his spine. His body stiffened.

Suddenly the fingers circled around to his side. The man let out a shriek.

"You're tickling!"

The woman laughed. She seemed to be teasing him, or else she was shy. It was too sudden; he could not pass judgment on the spur of the moment, What, really, was her intention? Had she done it on purpose or had her fingers slipped unintentionally? Until just a few minutes ago she had been blinking her eyes with all her might, trying to wake up. On the first night too, he recalled, she had laughed in that strange voice when she had jabbed him in the side as she passed by. He wondered whether she meant anything in particular by such conduct.

Perhaps she did not really believe in his pretended illness and was testing her suspicions. That was a possibility. He couldn't relax his guard. Her charms were like some meat-eating plant, purposely equipped with the smell of sweet honey. First she would sow the seeds of scandal by bringing him to an act of passion, and then the chains of blackmail would bind him hand and foot.

13

HE was melting away like wax. His pores were gorged with perspiration. Since his watch had stopped running, he was not sure of the hour. Outside this sixty-foot hole it might still be full daylight, but at the bottom it was already twilight.

The woman was still lost in sleep. Perhaps she was dreaming, for her arms and legs twitched nervously. He had tried to disturb her sleep, but he had failed. As for himself, he had slept enough.

He stood up and let the air strike his skin. The towel over his face had apparently fallen off when he turned in his sleep; so much sand had clung behind his ears, around his nostrils, and in the corners of his lips that he could scrape it off. He put some medicine in his eyes and covered them with the end of the towel; he repeated this several times and at length he was able to open them normally. But the eye medicine would be gone in two or three days. For that reason alone he wanted to bring things to a conclusion quickly. His body was as heavy as if he were lying on a magnetized bed in garments of iron. He made an effort to focus his eyes, and by the thin light that came through the door he blearily made out the newspaper print, like the legs of a dead fly.

Actually, he should have got the woman to read the paper to him in the daytime. That also would have disturbed her sleep: two birds with one stone. Too bad he had fallen asleep first. He had tried, but instead he had made a mess of things.

And tonight again he would curse that unbearable insomnia. He tried counting backwards from a hundred in rhythm with his breathing. Painstakingly he traced the road he was accustomed to walk from his boardinghouse to the school. He tried enumerating the names of all the insects he knew, grouping them by family and order. He was in far worse straits when he realized that all these devices had no effect at all. He could hear the sound of the wind sweeping over the edge of the hole . . . the lisp of the shovel cutting into the bed of wet sand . . . the distant barking of dogs . . . the faraway hum of voices, trembling like the flame of a candle. The ceaselessly pouring sand was like a file on the tips of his nerves. And yet, he must have the patience to endure it.

Well, somehow he would stand it. No sooner had the cooling blue light slipped down from the edge of the hole than everything was reversed, and he engaged in combat with sleep that sucked at him as a sponge sucks water. As long as this vicious circle was not broken somewhere, not only his watch but time itself would be immobilized, he feared, by the grains of sand.

The newspaper was the same as usual. He wondered if there had been a gap of a week, for there was almost nothing new to be found. If this was a window on the world outside, the glass was frosted.

Corporation Tax Bribery Spreads to City Officials. College Towns Become Industrial Meccas. Operations Suspended; General Labor Union Council to Meet Soon— Opinion to Be Published. Mother Strangles Two Children: Takes Poison. Do Frequent Auto Thefts Mean New Mode of Life Breeds New Crime? Unknown Girl Brings Flowers to Police Box for Three Years. Tokyo Olympics Budget Trouble. Phantom Stabs Two Girls Again Today. College Youths Poisoned by Sleeping Pill Spree. Stock Prices Feel Autumn Winds. Famous Tenor Sax, Blues Jackson, Arrives in Japan. Rioting Again in Union of South Africa—280 Fatalities. Co-ed Thieves

School Has No Tuition Fees—Graduation Certificate Issued on Successful Completion of Examination.

There wasn't a single item of importance. A tower of illusion, all of it, made of illusory bricks and full of holes. If life were made up only of important things, it really would be a dangerous house of glass, scarcely to be handled carelessly. But everyday life was exactly like the headlines. And so everybody, knowing the meaninglessness of existence, sets the center of his compass at his own home.

Suddenly his eyes fell on a surprising article.

About 8:00 A.M. on the fourteenth, at the East Asia Housing construction site, 30 Yokokawa-chō, a scoop-truck driver for the Hinohara Co., Mr. Tashiro Tsutomu (aged 28), received serious injuries when he was buried under a sand slide. He was taken to a nearby hospital but died shortly after arrival. According to the investigation carried out by the Yokokawa police, the cause of the accident appears to be that too much sand was removed from the lower part of a thirty-foot pile that was being leveled.

Aha! Doubtless this was the article that the villagers had intended him to see. They had not responded to his request for nothing. It was commendable that they had not circled the section in red ink. He was reminded of the dangerous weapon they called a blackjack. A blackjack is made by packing sand into a leather sack. It is said to have a striking power comparable to that of an iron or lead bar. No matter how sand flowed, it was still different from water. One could swim in water, but sand would enfold a man and crush him to death.

It looked as though he had misjudged the situation.

14

~~~~~~~~~~~~~~~~~~~~~~~~~~~~~

HE needed some time for thought before deciding on a new strategy. Four hours must have passed since the woman had gone out to clear away the sand. The second group of basket carriers had finished their appointed work and were returning in the direction of the three-wheeled truck. After he had made certain, straining his ears, that the men were not coming back, he quietly arose and put on his clothes. Since the woman had taken the lamp away with her, he had to do everything by touch. His shoes were brimful of sand. He tucked the cuffs of his trousers into his socks, then took out his leggings and thrust them into his pocket. He decided to gather his insect-collecting equipment together near the door so that he could find it easily. Thanks to the thick carpet of sand on the earthen floor, there was no need to be cautious about his footsteps.

The woman was completely preoccupied with her work. Her movements were smooth as she cut into the sand; her breathing was strong and regular. Her elongated shadow danced around the lamp at her feet. The man, concealing himself at the corner of the building, forced himself to breathe softly. In his hands he grasped the two ends of a towel and stretched it taut; after counting ten he would make a dash for it. His attack had to come at the instant she leaned forward to shovel up the heap of sand.

Of course, he could not pretend there was absolutely no danger. There was no telling—their attitude might suddenly change in a half hour. For instance, there was that government man. The old man from the village had at first mistaken him for the government man and shown signs of extreme caution. They must have expected the government man to make an inspection in the near future. If that were so, village opinion would split over him, and they might possibly give up keeping him prisoner and concealing his existence. But by the same token there was no guarantee that a half hour would not stretch into a half year, a year, or even more. It was a fifty-fifty chance whether it would be a year or a half hour, and he was certainly not ready to lay a wager.

When he considered that relief might be at hand, he realized that things would go better for him if he were to continue with his pretext of illness. But this was indeed the point that perplexed him. He lived under a constitutional government, and therefore it was natural that he should expect help. People who vanished in a fog of mystery and remained incommunicado frequently wanted to do just that. As long as the case didn't seem to be of a criminal nature, it would be entrusted to the civil rather than the criminal authorities, and thus even the police could not go too far into the matter.

But in his case the situation was completely different, and he was desperately reaching out for help. Anyone who saw his empty room would immediately understand what

had happened, even if they hadn't seen him or directly
heard from him. The unfinished book that lay open to the
page he had been reading when he put it down . . . the
small change he had tossed into the pocket of his office
clothes . . . his bankbook, which bore no trace of any
recent withdrawals, despite the small amount in his account . . . his box of drying insects he had not yet finished arranging . . . the stamped envelope containing the
order blank for a new collecting bottle, laid out ready for
mailing—all this repudiated discontinuance, everything
pointed to his intention to go on living. A visitor could not
help but hear the plaintive voice from the room.

Well . . . if it hadn't been for that letter . . . if it just
hadn't been for that stupid letter. Yet that was the point, it
had been. In his dream he had told the truth, but now he
was quibbling with himself. Why? He had made enough
excuses. Lost articles no longer existed. And he had long
since cut his throat with his own hands.

He had assumed an unreasonably mysterious attitude
about this holiday, saying nothing to any of his colleagues
about his intended destination. Not only had he left
without saying a word, but he had deliberately made a
point of the mystery. There couldn't be a more efficient
way of teasing his colleagues, glum and gray with their
daily gray routine. He sank into an unbearable self-aversion
with the thought that among the glum and gray, people
other than he had colors other than gray—red, blue, green.

It only happened in novels or movies that summer was
filled with dazzling sun. What existed in reality were hum-
ble, small-town Sundays . . . a man taking his snooze

under the political columns of a newspaper, enveloped in
gunsmoke . . . canned juices and thermos jugs with magnetized caps . . . boats for hire, fifty cents an hour—
queue up here . . . foaming beaches with the leaden scum
of dead fish . . . and then, at the end, a jam-packed trolley rickety with fatigue. Everyone knows this is fact, but
no one wants to make a fool of himself and be taken in;
so, on the gray canvas of reality, he zestfully sketches the
mere form of this illusory festival. Miserable, unshaven
fathers, shaking their complaining children by the shoulder
trying to make them say it has been a pleasant Sunday
. . . little scenes everyone has seen in the corner of some
trolley . . . people's pathetic jealousy and impatience
with others' happiness.

Well, if that were all, it was nothing to get so serious
about. If the Möbius man had not had the same reaction
as his other colleagues, it was doubtful whether he would
have been so obstinate.

He had tentatively trusted the man, a pop-eyed fellow,
who always looked as if he had just washed his face and
who was enthusiastic about unions. He had once sincerely
tried revealing his inner thoughts, which he seldom dis-
closed to anyone.

"What do you think? I have considerable doubt about a
system of education that imputes meaning to life."

"What do you mean by 'meaning'?"

"In other words, an illusory education that makes one
believe that something is when it really isn't. Therefore
I'm very interested in sand in this instance, because, even
though it's a solid, it has definite hydrodynamic properties."

The other, perplexed, had bent forward, arching his back like a cat. But his expression, as before, had remained open. He had not appeared to find the idea particularly unpleasant. Someone had once commented that the man resembled a Möbius strip. A Möbius strip is a length of paper, twisted once, the two ends of which are pasted together, thus forming a surface that has neither front nor back. Had they meant that this man's union life and his private life formed a Möbius circle? He remembered feeling a certain admiration for the man, and at the same time cynicism.

"In other words, do you mean realistic education?"

"No. The reason I brought up the example of sand was because in the final analysis I rather think the world is like sand. The fundamental nature of sand is very difficult to grasp when you think of it in its stationary state. Sand not only flows, but this very flow *is* the sand. I'm sorry I can't express it better."

"But I understand what you mean. Because in practical education you can't avoid getting involved in relativism, can you?"

"No, that's not it. You yourself become sand. You see with the eyes of sand. Once you're dead you don't have to worry about dying any more."

"You must be an idealist. I think you must be afraid of your students—aren't you?"

"I am, because I think my students are something like sand."

The man had laughed heartily, showing his white teeth, but not once had he appeared disturbed by the discordant exchange. His pop-eyes had quite disappeared between the folds of skin. Jumpei had not been able to repress a vague smile. The other was really quite like a Möbius circle. He was indeed a Möbius circle—in both a good and a bad sense. On the good face of it, he really deserved praise.

But, speaking of a Möbius circle, the other had frankly shown the same gray envy of his holiday as his colleagues had. It seemed a far cry from a Möbius circle. He was disappointed, but at the same time pleased. Anyone was apt to be ill-natured with virtue. And so, he had come, to take increasing pleasure in his teasing.

And then the letter . . . the irretrievable card that had already been delivered. The obsession in his dream the night before had had a very definite cause.

It would be false to claim that there was absolutely no love between him and the other woman. It was simply that theirs was a somewhat obscure relationship in which, mutually at odds as they were, he could never be sure of her. If, for example, he were to say that marriage was, in the final analysis, like cultivating undeveloped land, she would retort, angrily and unreasonably, that it meant having to make a cramped house bigger. Or, if he were to say the opposite, she would still take the contrary stand. It was a seesaw game that had been tirelessly repeated for a full two years and four months. Perhaps it would be better to say that, rather than losing their passion, they had frozen it by over-idealizing it.

And then he had decided quite suddenly to let her know by letter that he had gone off alone for a time and had purposely told no one of his destination. The mystery of his holiday, which would have such effect on his colleagues, would not produce any reaction from her. But he had thought the letter stupid and had tossed it, stamped and addressed, on his desk and come away.

This innocent act, as a result, was to be the automatic, thiefproof lock that only the owner could open. The letter was almost certain to catch someone's eye. It was as though he had purposely left a statement that he had disappeared of his own volition. He was just like some moronic criminal who, observed at the scene of his crime, had thereupon stupidly wiped away his fingerprints and thus proved his criminal intent.

His opportunity for escape receded into the distance. Yet, though he still clung to the possibility of rescue even now, his hopes would agonize in the poison of his doubts. Now the only way was to break open the doors by force without waiting for them to be opened. There was no excuse for hesitating any longer.

He dug his toes into the sand until they hurt, leaned forward, and prepared to spring out at the count of ten. But still he hesitated, even at the count of thirteen. At last, taking four deep breaths, he dashed out.

15

~~~~~~~~~~~~~~~~~~

In spite of his intention, his movements were sluggish, for his strength had been sapped by the sand. Already the woman had turned around and, with her shovel poised, was gazing at him in blank surprise.

If she really wanted to put up resistance, the result could be completely different from what he hoped. But his stratagem of taking her by surprise was completely successful. He had been too eager, but the woman was paralyzed. The thought of pushing him back with her poised shovel apparently never occurred to her.

"Don't cry out. I won't hurt you. Just keep quiet."

He kept whispering to her in a tense voice, haphazardly stuffing a towel into her mouth. She remained as he put her, without resisting—even in the face of this reckless, bungling act.

Finally he pulled himself together when he realized her passiveness. He withdrew the towel, which he had already half stuffed in, and rearranged it over her mouth, tying it firmly at the back of her neck. Then he bound her hands tightly behind her back with the leggings he had ready in his pocket.

"All right! Get in the house!"

The woman's spirit seemed greatly weakened, and she

was not only submissive to his acts but obedient to his words as well. She showed no resistance or antagonism. Perhaps she was in a kind of hypnotized state. He did not feel he had handled the situation particularly well, but his unexpected violence had apparently had the effect of taking all resistance out of her. He forced her up to the raised portion of flooring. And with the other legging he tied her legs together at the ankles. In the dark he had to proceed by feel, and just to be on the safe side he wrapped the remaining portion of the leggings once again around her ankles.

"Now, don't move! Do you understand? You won't get hurt as long as you behave yourself. But I'm desperate. . . ."

He kept looking in the direction of the woman's breathing as he backed away toward the door. From there, he dashed out, grabbed the shovel and the lamp, and ran back with them at once. The woman had fallen down on her side and was working her jaw up and down repeatedly as she breathed. She was probably pushing her jaw forward with each breath in order to avoid inhaling sand from the matting. And when she exhaled, on the other hand, she appeared to force the breath from her nose, thereby blowing the sand away from around her face.

"Well, you'll have to put up with this for a while. You'll have to be patient until the villagers come back with the baskets. There's no reason for you to complain after the nonsense I've had to put up with. Besides, I'll pay honest board. Of course, only the actual expenses I calculate myself. You can't mind that, can you? Really, my stay here should be free, but I can't stand not canceling such a debt. I'm going to make you take it."

For some time, nervous and agitated, holding out his collar to let in the air, he strained his ears for signs of life outside. Yes, it might be better to extinguish the lamp. He lifted the chimney and was about to blow—but no, before that he had better check on the woman. The knots were tight enough on her legs; there was not even room to insert a finger. Her wrists were already swollen a dark red, and her spatulate fingernails had turned the color of an old ink smear.

The gag too was perfect. She had drawn her dull-colored lips so taut there was almost no blood in them, and she appeared almost ghostly. Saliva dribbled out of her mouth and made a dark stain on the matting under her cheek. With the wavering of the lamp he seemed to hear her voiceless screams.

"It's no use. You started the whole thing yourself anyway," he said quickly without thinking. "We've tried to get the best of each other, and we're about even, aren't we? I'm human too, and you can't simply tie me up like a dog. Anybody would call it legitimate self-defense on my part."

Suddenly the woman twisted her neck and tried to catch sight of him out of the corner of her half-closed eyes.

"What's wrong? Do you want to say something?"

She moved her neck awkwardly. It was as if she were nodding assent, or even dissent. He drew the lamp closer and tried to read her eyes. He could not immediately believe what he saw. They were filled with infinite sorrow, in which there was neither bitterness nor hatred, and she seemed to be appealing for something.

Impossible. It must be his own imagination. "Expression

in the eyes" is really only a figure of speech. How can expression exist in an eyeball that has no muscle? Even so, he winced and stretched out his hands to loosen the gag.

He drew them back and hastily blew out the lamp. The voices of the basket carriers were drawing close. He placed the darkened lamp on the edge of the ramp around the raised portion of the floor so that he could find it easily and, putting his lips to the kettle under the sink, took a drink of water. With the shovel clutched in his hands, he concealed himself by the door. He began to perspire. It would be soon now. He would have to be patient for five or ten minutes more. With one hand he drew his collecting box close to him.

16

"Hey, there!" A hoarse voice rang out.

"What are you doing down there?" Another voice, vibrant and still young, echoed the first.

The man was enclosed in the palpable darkness of the hole. But outside, the moon had evidently risen, and the shadows of men on the line between the sand and the sky were an indistinct, expanding blob.

He edged closer, hugging the bottom of the hole, his shovel in his right hand.

A coarse laugh sounded at the top of the cliff. A rope,

with a hook for the kerosene cans, was being lowered hand over hand.

"Come on, lady. Get a move on!"

At that very instant the man sprang toward the rope, kicking up the sand as he ran.

"Hey, there! Pull 'er up!" He shouted as loud as he could, clinging to the taut rope with a grip that would have sunk his fingers into stone. "Pull 'er up! Pull 'er up! I won't let go until you do! I've tied the woman up in the house. If you want to help her, hoist the rope right away. I won't let you get to the woman until you do! And if you happen to come down here I'll split your brains open with this shovel. Just take me to court and see who'll win. Do you really expect me to make allowances for you? What are you fussing around for? If you haul me right up I'll withdraw my complaint and overlook the whole thing. Illegal detention is no light crime. What's the matter? Get a move on and pull me up!"

The sand that poured down struck his face. A cold, clammy feeling was rapidly spreading from his collar into his shirt. His hot breath burned his lips.

Above, it seemed they had begun some sort of discussion. Suddenly there was a strong pull, and they began to haul the rope up. His inert weight, heavier than he had expected, ripped the rope through his fingers. He clung on with redoubled strength. A violent spasm like laughter convulsed his stomach. It was as if the week's nightmare had broken into pieces and flown asunder. Good. . . . Good. . . . He was saved!

Suddenly he was weightless and floating in space. A feeling of nausea, as though he were seasick, passed through his body, and the rope which until then had wrenched at his arms lay passive in his hands.

The gang above had let go! He made a backward somersault and was thrown out on the sand. Under him his insect box gave out an unpleasant sound. And something grazed his cheek—apparently the hook at the end of the rope. The bastards! Fortunately he was uninjured. When he inspected his side, where he had struck the insect box, he found there was no particular place that hurt. He jumped up at once, looking around for the rope. It had already been drawn up.

"Stupid fools!"

He shouted brokenly, in a hoarse voice. "Stupid fools! You're the ones who are going to be sorry in the end!"

There was no response. Only a silent murmuring drifted over him like smoke. It annoyed him more and more, for he was unable to decide whether it was a hostile sound or whether they were merely stifling their laughter.

His anger and humiliation were a hard core of iron inside him. He continued to shout, sinking his nails into his sweaty palms.

"Don't you understand me? I didn't think you would if I just told you in words. Didn't I make myself clear by what I did? Didn't I tell you I've tied the woman up? You'd better haul me up right away. The woman stays the way she is until you hand over the rope ladder. There's nobody to clear away the sand. Is that all right with you? Think it over. You're going to be the ones in trouble if we're buried by the sand. If the sand gets over here it will gradually force its way through the whole village. What's wrong? Why don't you answer?"

In place of an answer the men had simply left in a disappointingly offhanded way, leaving behind them only the sound of their trailing baskets.

"Why? Why do you go off like that without saying a word?" he cried out weakly, but the sound of his voice was audible only to himself. Trembling, he bent over and gathered up the contents of his collecting box. It looked as if there was a crack in his alcohol container, and the instant his hand touched it a fresh coolness spread between his fingers. He sobbed in a stifled voice. But he was not particularly sad. He felt quite as if someone else were crying.

The sand clung to him like some crafty animal. Then, feeling his way with difficulty, he tottered in the dark to the doorway and went into the house. He gently placed his unhinged collecting box by the side of the sunken fireplace. The sound of a roaring wind filled the air. He took out the plastic-wrapped matches from the empty can in the corner of the fireplace and lit the lamp.

The woman's position had not changed; she had only shifted the angle of her body down a little. She turned her face slightly in the direction of the door, perhaps with the intention of checking on the situation outside, blinked an instant at the light, but at once closed her eyes tightly again. He wondered just how she would take the cold-blooded treatment he had received. If she wanted to cry, let her cry; if she wanted to laugh, let her laugh. It was not yet a foregone conclusion that he had lost the game. In any case, he was the one who held the fuse to the time bomb.

He knelt down on one knee behind the woman. He hesitated an instant and then released the gag and tore it off. He did not feel particularly guilty. He had not the slightest feeling of pity or compassion.

He was simply worn out. He could not stand any more strain. Furthermore, when he thought about it, the gag had not been necessary from the first. If the woman had cried out for help at that time, she would have thrown him into a panic and would perhaps have hastened the outcome of the matter.

She thrust out her jaw, panting. The towel was as heavy as a dead rat with her saliva and foul breath. It had bitten into her flesh, leaving freckled spots, which did not seem about to go away. The stiffness in her cheeks, which had become like the skin of dried fish, began to relax as she repeatedly moved her lower jaw. "You'll soon be all right," he said, picking up the towel by the tips of his fingers and throwing it toward the earthen floor. "It's about time for them to have come to some decision. They'll certainly bring the rope ladder pretty fast now. They're the ones that are going to be in trouble if they let things go on as they are. And that's the truth. There was no need at all for them to go to the trouble of trapping me if they didn't have to."

The woman swallowed her sour spittle and moistened her lips.

"But . . ." Her tongue did not seem to have regained its functioning. She spoke in a muffled voice as if she were holding an egg in her mouth. "Have the stars come out?"

"The stars? Why the stars?"

"Well, it's just that if the stars aren't out . . ."

"What do you mean, if they're not out?"

But she was exhausted with this much talk and again sank into silence.

"What's wrong? You can't stop in the middle of what you started to say! Are you going to tell my horoscope or something? Or is it a superstition in this part of the country? I suppose they don't let the rope ladder down on starless nights. What about it? Eh? I can't understand you if you don't say anything. If you want to wait until the stars come out, it's up to you. But what'll you do if a strong wind comes up while you're waiting? The last thing you'll think of is stars!"

"If the stars don't come out by this time," she said in a voice that sounded as if it had been squeezed out of a worn-out tube, "there won't be a very strong wind."

"Why?"

"If you can't see the stars, it's because there's mist."

"What do you mean by saying such a thing when the wind is blowing as hard as it is?"

"No. That's the rush of the wind way up above."

He thought about this; it might well be as she said. The fact that the stars were obscured meant, after all, that the wind did not have the power to blow away the vapors in the atmosphere. There would probably not be much of a wind tonight. If that were the case, the villagers would probably not press things to a conclusion. What he had taken to be downright nonsense had turned out in fact to be a surprisingly logical answer.

"Of course. But I'm not at all worried. If it's their idea to hold out, it'll be a battle of nerves. It's six of one and half a dozen of the other whether I wait a week, ten days, or even fifteen."

The woman curled her toes tightly inward. They looked like the suction cups of a suckfish. He laughed. And as he was laughing he became nauseated.

Why in heaven's name was he on tenterhooks like this? He was the one who was pressing on the enemy's vulnerable spot, wasn't he? Why couldn't he observe things in a more self-possessed way? If and when he got back safely it would certainly be well worth while setting down this experience.

—Well, Niki, I am amazed. At last you have decided to write something. It really was the experience that made you. A common earthworm won't attain full growth if it's not stimulated, they say.

—Thanks. Actually I've got to think up some kind of title.

—Hmm. What kind, I wonder? "The Devil of the Sands" or "The Terrors of an Ant Hell"?

—They show a terrible taste for the bizarre. Don't they give much too insincere an impression?

—Do you think so?

—It's meaningless, no matter how intense the experience, to trace only the surface of the event. The heroes of this tragedy are the local boys, and if you don't give some hint of the solution by describing them, your rare experience will be lost. . . . Pew!

—What is it?

—Are they cleaning the sewers somewhere? Or maybe

it's some special chemical reaction between the garlic smell in your mouth and the antiseptic solution they're using to scrub the corridor.

—What?

—No, take it easy. No matter how I try to write I'm not fit to be a writer.

—This unbecoming humility again. There's no need for you to think of writers as something special. If you write, you're a writer, aren't you?

—Well, it's generally considered that teachers are prone to write indiscriminately.

—But professionally they're pretty close to writers.

—Is that what they call creative education? . . . In spite of the fact that they haven't even made a pencil box by themselves?

—A pencil box . . . how impressive! Isn't it good to be made to realize what sort of person one is?

—Thanks to this education, I have to experience a new sensation in order to appreciate new pain.

—There's hope.

—But one is not responsible for whether the hope materializes or not.

—From that point on, one has to try to put one's faith in one's own power.

—All right, let's stop the self-deception. Such a vice is impermissible in any teacher.

—Vice?

—That's for writers. Saying you want to become a writer is no more than egotism; you want to distinguish between yourself and the puppets by making yourself a puppeteer.

What difference is there really between this and a woman's using make-up?

—That's severe. But if you use the term "writer" in such a sense, certainly you should be able to distinguish to a certain extent between being a writer and writing.

—Ah. You see! That's the very reason I wanted to become a writer. If I couldn't be a writer there would be no particular need to write!

He must look like a child who has not received his allowance.

17

From the lower face of the cliff came an abrupt sound like the flapping of wings. He grabbed the lamp and rushed out. A package wrapped in matting was lying in the sand. There was not a sign of anyone around. He shouted in a loud voice. There was no answer at all. With eager curiosity he snatched away the rope fastened around the matting. He could only suppose that the package contained implements for climbing the cliff. The villagers still could not show their faces; they had only thrown the things down to him and fled, he supposed.

But the contents were only a pint bottle with a wooden stopper and a small package wrapped in a sheet of newspaper. In the package were three boxes, each containing twenty Shinsei cigarettes. Nothing more. He grasped the edges of the matting again and shook it violently, but only sand spilled out. He had counted on some scrap of a letter at least, but there was nothing. The bottle contained cheap saké that smelled of rice mold.

Whatever could they be about? Could they be bargaining? He had heard that the Indians of America exchanged cigarettes as a sign of friendship. And, in Japan, saké too was commonly a part of some happy occasion. Thus it was certainly plausible to suppose that their actions were a sort of advance expression of their intention to come to an agreement. Country people tended to be self-conscious about expressing their feelings in words. And in this sense they were more honest.

He acquiesced for the time being; cigarettes were more important than anything else. How had he ever stood being without them for over a week? With an accustomed gesture he broke the label and stripped it off squarely down the side. It felt like smooth wax paper. He snapped the bottom and forced a cigarette out. The fingers that held it trembled. He took a light from the lamp, filling his lungs with slow, deep breaths, and the fragrance penetrated his blood to the farthest corner of his body. His lips felt numb, and a heavy velvet curtain descended over his eyes. He felt a dizziness as if he were being strangled, and a chill went through him.

Clutching the pint bottle tightly to him, he reeled back to the house on faraway legs that were not his own. His head was still firmly clamped in a hoop of dizziness. He tried to look over at the woman, but no matter how he tried he

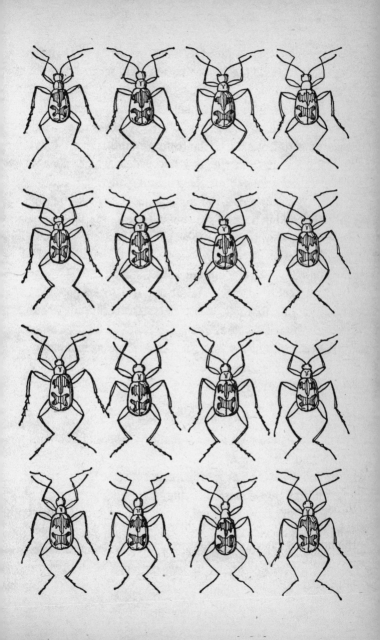

could not see straight ahead. Her face, which he had caught diagonally out of the corner of one eye, seemed terribly small.

"It's a present. See." He held the pint bottle up and shakily showed it to her. "Aren't they considerate! They gave us a full one to celebrate in advance. Didn't I tell you? I knew it from the very first. Well, what's done is done. What about a snort? Keep me company?"

Instead of answering the woman closed her eyes tightly. Was she sulking because she couldn't get him to loosen her ropes? Stupid woman! If she would give him one good answer he would probably release her right away. Was she moping because she could not keep the man she had gone to such trouble to catch and at last had to let go? That might be true too. . . . After all, she was still only about thirty . . . and a widow.

Between the instep and the back of the woman's foot there was a conspicuous and disagreeable fold. Again, a nonsensical laugh welled up in him. Why was her foot that funny?

"If you want a cigarette I'll give you a light, shall I?"

"No. Cigarettes make my throat dry," she said in a faint voice, shaking her head.

"Well, then, shall I give you a drink of water?"

"I'm all right for the time being."

"You don't have to be polite. You know I didn't subject you to this because of any personal dislike for you. You understand, don't you, that strategically it was unavoidable? Your predicament seems to have softened the others up there a little."

"They deliver cigarettes and saké once a week to places where men are working, anyway."

"What do you mean they deliver?" He was a big black fly that thought it had taken flight when it was only bumping its head against the windowpane in its effort to get out. (The scientific name is *Muscina stabulans*.) Such flies have compound eyes with almost no power of sight. Without even trying to conceal his dismay, he shouted in a shrill voice: "But they don't have to go to such trouble for us! Can't they let us out to buy them ourselves?"

"But the work's hard and we don't have that much time. Besides, we're working for the village, and it's up to the village association to take care of the expenses."

Well then, far from compromise, they were perhaps advising him to give up! No, it was much worse, he thought. He had doubtless already been entered in the register alongside many others as a mere cog in the working of their everyday life.

"Just to satisfy myself, I'd like to ask you a little question: Am I the first, up until now, to have had an experience like this?"

"No. . . . Anyway, we don't have enough help. The ones who can work—like property owners, poor people, anybody—leave the village one after the other. Anyway, it's a poor village. All there is is sand. . . ."

"Then what's to become of it?" he said in a quiet voice that had taken on the protective coloring of sand. "There's somebody else you caught besides me, isn't there?"

"Yes, there is. It must have been in early autumn last year, I think . . . the postcard dealer. . . ."

"The postcard dealer?"

"The salesman or something from a company that makes postcards and other things for tourists came to visit the head of the local union. He told us that if we really advertised the beautiful scenery to people in the cities . . ."

"And you caught him?"

"A house on the same side as mine was having trouble with help at the time."

"Well, what happened then?"

"They say he died soon afterward. I understand he wasn't very strong to start with. Besides, it happened to be the typhoon season, and the work was extra hard."

"Why didn't he escape right away?"

The woman did not answer. Perhaps it was so self-evident that there was no need to. He hadn't escaped because he couldn't. That was probably all there was to it.

"Anyone else?"

"Yes. Some time after the beginning of the year, let me see, there was a student going around selling books or something."

"A peddler?"

"They were thin books, I remember, about ten yen, and they were against something."

"Ah, a Back-to-the-Land student. You know. They used to go around the countryside whipping up support for their anti-American campaigns. Did you catch him too?"

"He must still be at my neighbor's, three houses down."

"And of course they took away the rope ladder?"

"The younger ones don't settle down very well, that's why. I suppose it's because in town the pay is good, and then the movies, and restaurants, and stores are open every day."

"But hasn't a single one succeeded in escaping from here yet?"

"Well, yes. There was a young fellow who went to town and got into bad company. He was pretty big with his knife . . . it even came out in the papers . . . and then after he finished his time they brought him back, and now I think he's living quietly with his parents."

"I'm not asking about such people. I'm asking about those who don't come back once they've escaped!"

"It was a long time ago, but there was a whole family that managed to get out during the night, I remember. The house was vacant for a long time and got to be dangerous and beyond repair. It's really dangerous. If any one place along the dunes gives way, then it's like a dike with a hole in it."

"You mean there was nobody after that?"

"No. Not a one, I think."

"Absurd!" The blood vessels under his ears swelled, and his throat tightened.

The woman suddenly doubled up like a wasp laying eggs.

"What's wrong? Are you in pain?"

"Yes. Oh, these things hurt."

He felt the back of her hands, which had become discolored. He slipped his fingers through the cords that bound her and felt her pulse.

"You feel that, don't you? The pulse is strong. It doesn't seem to be serious. Sorry, but I'd like to have you tell your complaints to the ones in the village who are responsible for this."

"I'm sorry to bother you, but would you just scratch the place on my neck behind my ear?"

Taken by surprise, he could not refuse. There was a thick layer of perspiration like melted butter between her skin and the layer of sand. It felt as though he had put his nails on a peach.

"I'm really sorry. But honestly there hasn't been a single person to get out yet."

Suddenly the outline of the doorway became a faint, colorless line and floated away. It was the moon . . . a fragment of wan light like the wings of an ant. As his eyes became accustomed to it, the whole bottom of the sand bowl turned into a lustrous liquid that had the texture of new foliage.

"All right, then! I'll be the first to get out!"

18

It was hard to wait. Time was folded in endless, deep, bellows-like pleats. If he did not pause at each fold he could not go ahead. And in every fold there were all kind of suspicions, each clutching its own weapon. It took a terrible effort to go ahead, disputing or ignoring these doubts or casting them aside.

Finally, after he had waited the whole night through, dawn came. The morning, pressing its face, like the belly of a snail, against the windowpane, was laughing at him.

"Excuse me, but may I have some water?"

He must have fallen into a light sleep. His shirt and his trousers down to the backs of his knees were soaked with perspiration. The sand, clinging to the perspiration, was like a soggy wheat cake in texture and color. Since he had forgotten to cover his face, his nose and mouth were as dry as a winter paddy field.

"I'm sorry, but please . . . can I . . . ?"

The woman's whole body trembled under a cover of hardened sand, and she emitted a dry sound as if she had a fever. Her suffering was transmitted directly to him as if they had been connected by electric wires. He took the plastic cover off the kettle and jammed the spout into his mouth. He tried rinsing with the first mouthful, but it was impossible to clear his mouth with so little water. Only lumps of sand came out. Then, not caring, he let the sand run down his throat along with the water. It was as if he were drinking pebbles.

The water he drank poured out at once in perspiration. The skin on his back, around his chest, and on his sides down to his hips pained him as though a thin layer of it had been stripped away. Almost apologetically he pressed the spout of the kettle to the woman's lips. She took it between her teeth and, without rinsing her mouth, gulped the water down, cooing like a pigeon. Three good swallows and the kettle was empty. For the first time an unforgiving, reproachful look appeared in her eyes as she stared fixedly at him from beneath her swollen eyelids. The empty kettle felt light, as if it were made of folded paper.

The man stepped down on the earthen floor, dusting the sand from his body in an attempt to relieve the disagreeable feeling. Should he try to wipe the woman's face with a wet towel? That would make more sense than to let the perspiration go on running down until she was soaked. They say the level of civilization is proportionate to the degree of cleanliness of the skin. Assuming that man has a soul, it must, in all likelihood, be housed in the skin. These musings on water led him to realize that dirty skin had thousands and thousands of suction cups. Skin was coolly transparent, like ice . . . a soft, downlike bandage for the soul. If he waited an instant longer the skin of his whole body would rot away and peel off.

He looked into the water jar and let out a cry of dismay.

"My God! Do you realize it's empty? It's completely empty!"

He thrust his arm into the jar and stirred around. The dark sand which clung to the bottom scarcely stained his fingertips. Under his disappointed skin a thousand wounded centipedes began to struggle.

"The bastards forgot to deliver water. I even wonder if they intend bringing any more."

He knew very well that he had said this just to console himself. The three-wheeled truck always finished its last job and went back a little before daybreak. He realized what the rascals were up to. They were probably trying to make him howl by cutting off the water supply when there was none left. He thought it over and realized that they were the kind who would have let him go on, knowing full well how dangerous it was to cut away the cliff from the bottom. Definitely, they had little sympathy for him. Certainly they would never let a person get back alive who knew this much of their secret, and if that were the case, they probably intended going all the way.

He stood in the doorway and looked up at the sky. At last he could distinguish the red tints of the morning sun. Small fleecy clouds . . . not patterns that promised rain. It seemed that with each breath he exhaled, his body lost more moisture.

"What in God's name do they think they're doing? Do they want to kill me?"

The woman continued to tremble as usual. Perhaps it was because she knew all about what was happening. After all, she was an accomplice who had assumed the stance of an aggrieved party. Let her suffer. It was fitting retribution for her to suffer like this.

But it would serve no purpose if he didn't let the villagers know of her suffering. And there was no assurance that they would know about it. He knew very well that, far from taking pity on her, they would sacrifice the woman without compunction if the need arose. Perhaps that was the reason she was frightened. He was like an animal who finally sees that the crack in the fence it was trying to escape through is in reality merely the entrance to its cage—like a fish who at last realizes, after bumping its nose numberless times, that the glass of the goldfish bowl is a wall. For a second time he was flung down with no defense. Now the other side held the arms.

But he must not be frightened. When a castaway collapses from hunger and thirst it is a fear of physical want rather than a real want, they say. Defeat begins with the fear that one has lost. Perspiration dripped from the tip of his nose. If he was worrying about how many cubic centimeters of moisture he was losing with every drop, he had already fallen into the enemy's trap. It would be interesting to speculate just how long it would take for a glass of water to evaporate. Unnecessary fussing would not make time go faster.

"How about it? Shall I loosen the ropes?"

The woman held her breath suspiciously.

"I don't care if you don't want me to. If you want me to, I'll loosen them. But there's one condition: don't take up the shovel under any circumstances without my permission. How about it? Will you promise me that?"

"Oh, please!" The woman, who had been like a patient dog, began begging with the abruptness of an umbrella turned inside out by a sudden gust of wind. "I'll promise you anything. Please! Oh, please!"

The ropes had left black-and-blue marks, on the surface of which was a whitish, sodden film. She lay as she was, with her face up, rubbing her ankles together. Then, grasping her wrists, she began to loosen the cords one by one. She ground her teeth together trying not to cry out, and perspiration broke out in spots on her face. Gradually she turned her body and, lifting her buttocks, got up on all fours. Last of all, with much effort, she lifted her head. For some time she swayed back and forth in the same position.

The man sat quietly on the ramp around the raised portion of the floor. He forced out some saliva and swallowed it. He repeated the action, and the saliva became glutinous like paste and stuck in his throat. Of course, he did not feel like sleeping, but his fatigued senses had become like wet paper. The landscape floated before him in dirty patches and lines. It was really a picture-puzzle landscape. There was a woman . . . there was sand . . . there was an empty water jar . . . there was a drooling wolf . . . there was a sun. And, somewhere, he knew not where, there must also be a storm center and lines of discontinuity. Where in God's name should he start on this equation filled with unknowns?

The woman stood up and slowly walked toward the door.

"Where are you going?"

She mumbled something as if avoiding him, and he could hardly catch what she had said. But he understood her embarrassment. At length, from just beyond the board wall, came a quiet sound of urinating. Somehow everything seemed futile.

19

How true. Time cannot be spurred on like a horse. But it is not quite so slow as a pushcart. Gradually the morning temperature attained its usual intensity; his eyeballs and brain began to seethe; the heat pierced his innards; his lungs burned.

The moisture that the sand had absorbed during the night became vapor and was belched back into the atmosphere. The sand gave out a light which, through the refracted sunshine, made it seem like wet asphalt. Yet basically it remained the unadulterated ⅛ mm., drier than plain flour baked in a tin.

Soon came the first sand slide. It was a noise he was used to, one that had become a part of the daily routine, but involuntarily he and the woman exchanged glances. What would be the consequences of having let the sand go for a day? While he did not think they would be serious, he was still worried. But the woman turned her eyes away in silence. Her sulky look gave the impression that he could worry alone as he pleased. He'd be damned if he'd ask her any more. Just when the sand slide seemed to thin out to a thread, it widened again to the size of a belt; it repeated the process by fits and starts and at length quietly ceased.

It certainly did not seem serious enough to worry about. He heaved a sigh; the pulse pounded in his face, and he felt a burning sensation. The thought of the cheap saké, which he had tried not to think about until then, suddenly began to draw his nerves to a point, like a flame floating in darkness. Anything would be all right; he wanted to moisten his throat. If he let things go on as they were, the blood in his body would dwindle away. He knew full well that he was sowing the seeds of his suffering and that later he would regret it, but he could resist no longer. He took out the stopper, thrust the bottle to his lips, and drank. Yet his tongue, like a faithful watchdog surprised by an unexpected intruder, set up a howl. He choked. It was like sprinkling alcohol on a cut. Nonetheless, he could not control a desire for a second and even a third swallow. What horrible saké!

Since the woman was there he offered her some too. Of course, she declined. Her refusal was as exaggerated as if he were forcing her to take poison.

As he had feared, the alcohol in his stomach bounced to his head like a ping-pong ball, ringing like the buzz of a bee in his ears. His skin began to stiffen like pig's hide. His blood was spoiling! . . . His blood was dying away!

"Can't you do anything? It must be hard enough for you too. I loosened your ropes, so do something!"

"All right. But if I don't get somebody from the village to bring water . . ."

"Well, why don't you get them to?"

"I could . . . if we were just to start working. . . ."

"Don't be funny! Where do those fellows get the right to strike such an absurd bargain? Just tell me that! You can't, can you? They don't have the right, and you know it!"

The woman lowered her eyes and was silent. What a situation. The sky, visible above the door, had changed from blue to a glaring white, like the underside of a seashell. Granted that obligation is a man's passport among his fellow men, why did he have to get a permit from the villagers? Human life shouldn't be so many bits of paper scattered about. Life is a bound diary, and one first page is plenty for one book. There is no need to do one's duty for a page that is unrelated to the preceding ones. One can't get involved every time someone else is on the point of starvation. Damn it! He wanted water. But no matter how much he wanted water, he still did not have enough bodies to go around to all the funeral services of people who were of no consequence to him.

A second sand slide began.

The woman stood up and took down a broom from the wall.

"You can't work! You promised, didn't you?"

"No, no. It's for the mattresses. . . ."

"The mattresses?"

"If you don't get some sleep pretty soon . . ."

"If I get sleepy, I'll take care of them myself."

He felt an earth-shaking shock and stood rooted to the ground. For a moment everything seemed misty with sand that fell from the ceiling. The consequences of having stopped the shoveling were at last apparent. The sand, having no way out, was bearing down. The joints of the beams and uprights groaned in agony. But the woman, staring fixedly at an inner lintel, did not appear particularly concerned. The pressure still seemed to be only around the base of the house.

"Damn them! Do they really intend going on like this forever?"

His racing heart! It was hopping about like a frightened rabbit, as if unable to stay in its own hole. It seemed ready to crawl in anywhere—his mouth, his ears, or even into his bowel. His spittle had become much more viscid. And the dryness in his throat was as bad. Perhaps it was because his thirst had not been adequately slaked by the cheap saké. As soon as the alcohol was dissipated, it would flare up again, and the flames would reduce him to ashes.

"They must feel fine . . . doing such things. They don't have the brains of a mouse. Just what would they do if I died?"

The woman raised her face as if to say something but, suddenly thinking better of it, maintained her unbroken silence. She apparently did not think it worthwhile to answer at all.

All right. If there was to be only one inevitable ending anyway, why didn't he try whatever he could?

He gulped down another mouthful from the bottle of saké and, bracing himself, hurried outside. He reeled back as if molten lead had struck his eyes. The sand, which spilled over into the hollows left by his feet, eddied in whirlpools. Over there was surely the place he had attacked the woman and tied her up the night before. The shovel must surely be buried nearby. The sand slide had mostly stopped for a while, but even so, on the cliff toward the sea, the sand continued its ceaseless flow. From time to time, blown by the wind, it would drop from the face of the cliff, fluttering like a piece of cloth. Taking care not to start a slide, he fished around with the toes of one foot.

Although he probed deeply, his foot met no resistance at all. The direct rays of the sun soon became unbearable. The pupils of his eyes were compressed to pin points, and his belly began to throb like a jellyfish. A violent pain pierced his forehead. He must not lose any more perspiration. This was the limit. He wondered what he could have done with the shovel. He had taken it out with the intention of using it as a weapon; that was certain. So it must be around. Peering closely at the surface of the ground, he was suddenly aware that at one point the sand was standing out in a ridge in the form of the shovel.

He began to spit but hastily stopped himself. He must retain in his body even the slightest bit of moisture. He separated the spittle from the sand between his teeth and his lips and with the end of his finger scraped off only the portion that remained clinging to his teeth.

The woman, facing the other way in a corner of the room, was doing something with the front of her kimono. Perhaps she was unloosening her waistband or brushing off the sand which had accumulated. He grasped the shovel halfway down the handle and brought it up to the level of his shoulders. Aiming at the wall that surrounded the earthen floor, near the doorway, he heaved to with the cutting edge.

The woman cried out behind him. He lunged with the shovel, bearing on it with all his weight. Disappointingly, it passed through the wall boards. They had the resistance of a wet cracker. Washed by the sand, they had seemed quite new from the outside, but it was apparent they had already begun to disintegrate.

"What are you doing?"

"I'm stripping this stuff off to make some material for a ladder."

He experimented again at another spot. It was the same. Apparently the woman had been right when she said that the sand rotted the wood. If the part of the wall that was most exposed to the sun was like this, he could imagine what the rest would be like. It was remarkable that such a flabby house could be standing at all. It was bent and warped as if paralyzed on one side. Maybe such flimsy structures were dynamically possible, since they seemed to be making houses out of plastic and paper these days, but . . .

If that was the way it was with the boards, then he would try the cross-beams.

"You can't do that! Stop! Please!"

"After all, we're going to be crushed by the sand anyway."

Without paying any attention, he poised his arm to strike, but the woman, screaming, rushed violently at him. He put out his elbow and twisted his body in an effort to ward her off. But he had miscalculated, and instead of the woman he himself was swung around. Instantly he tried to counter, but she held on as if chained to the shovel. He did not understand. At least he could not be defeated by force. They rolled over two or three times, threshing about on the earthen floor, and for a brief moment he thought he had pinned her down, but with the handle of the shovel as a shield she deftly flipped him over. Something was wrong with him; maybe it was the saké he had drunk. Anyway, he no longer cared that his opponent was a woman. He jabbed his bended knee into her stomach.

The woman cried out, and suddenly her strength ebbed. At once he rolled over on her and held her down. Her breasts were bare, and his hands slipped on skin that was slippery with sweat.

Suddenly the two of them froze, as in a movie when the

projector breaks down. It was a petrified moment that would go on and on, if one of them did not do something. He could sense vividly the structure of her breasts outlined against his stomach, and his penis seemed like a living thing completely independent of him. He held his breath. With a slight turn of his body the scramble for the shovel would turn into something very different.

The woman's gorge rose as she tried to swallow the saliva in her mouth. His penis received this as a signal to stir, but she interrupted in a husky voice.

"City women are all pretty, aren't they?"

"City women?" He was suddenly ashamed. The fever in his swollen member was abating. They seemed to have skirted the danger with good grace. He had not realized that soap opera could survive even in the midst of sand.

Yet the average woman was firmly convinced, it seemed, that she could not make a man recognize her worth unless every time she opened her legs she did so as if it were a scene in a soap opera. But this very pathetic and innocent illusion in fact made women the victims of a one-sided, spiritual rape.

With his other woman, he had decided he would always use a condom. Even now he was not convinced that he had been completely cured of the venereal disease he had once had. The results of the tests always came out negative, but after urinating his urethra would suddenly begin to hurt, and when he checked a sample in a test tube, there would be, just as he had feared, something floating around in it, something resembling a piece of waste thread. The doctor had diagnosed it as a nervous disturbance, but he could not get rid of the suspicion that it was still the same old trouble.

"Well, a rubber suits us pretty well, doesn't it?" Her small jaws and lips were covered with a thin skin, through which the blood seemed to be visible. She spoke with a certain calculated spite: "Between us it's like buying at a department store, isn't it? If you don't like it, you can take it back any time. You make your mind up, looking at something wrapped up in plastic—you can look without breaking the seal. You wonder what's inside. You wonder if you can trust it. You wonder if you won't be sorry later if you buy the wrong thing now."

But in her heart she was probably not satisfied with such a commercial-sample type of relationship. . . . He remembered the brothel smell of disinfectant as he had begun buttoning up his trousers, already feeling he was being hurried out . . . and the woman still naked on the bed with the towel stuck between her legs.

"But it's all right if once in a while you feel like forcing a sale, isn't it?"

"No, it isn't. Any forcing . . ."

"But you're cured by now, aren't you?"

"If you really think that, then why don't we agree to go on without protection?"

"Come on, now. Why are you trying to get out of your responsibilities?"

"Well, didn't I say I don't like to force a sale?"

"It's very strange. What have I got to do with your venereal disease, for heaven's sake?"

"Maybe you do have something to do with it."

"Don't be silly!"

"Well, anyway, I withdraw the forced selling."

"Well then, don't you ever intend to take off your hat in your whole life?"

"I wonder why you're so uncooperative. It would be natural for you to feel tender toward me if we slept together."

"In other words, you've got a psychological veneral disease, haven't you? By the way, maybe I'll have to work tomorrow."

Hmm. A psychological venereal disease, he thought, yawning. It's a pretty clever expression for her to think up. But she would never know just how much the expression had hurt him. In the first place, venereal disease was the exact opposite of soap opera. Venereal disease was the most desperate evidence that soap opera did not exist. Venereal disease . . . stealthily imported by Columbus in his tiny ships into tiny harbors . . . spread so diligently by everyone throughout the world. All men were equal before death and venereal disease. Venereal disease . . . the collective responsibility of mankind. Nevertheless, she absolutely refused to admit it. She had shut herself in her own Alice in Wonderland tale where she herself played the main role. And he was left alone on this side of the mirror, suffering with his psychological venereal disease. And so his naked—hatless—member was paralyzed and useless. Her mirror made him impotent. Her woman's innocence had turned him into an enemy.

20

~~~~~~~~~~~~~~~~~

His face was as stiff as starch, his breathing like a storm.
His saliva tasted of dry scorched sugar . . . and such a terrible loss of energy. At least one glassful of water must
have evaporated in perspiration. The woman arose slug-
gishly, keeping her head bent. Her sand-streaked face
came to about the height of his eyes. Suddenly she blew her
nose with her fingers and rubbed her hands with sand that
she scooped up. Her trousers slipped down over her bending
hips.

Annoyed, he turned his eyes away. Yet it was not quite
right to say he was only annoyed. A strange feeling, different from dryness, lingered on the tip of his tongue. His
member had been pulsating and vibrant without the rubber, although only for a short time, until he had been put
off by the woman's stupid expression. And now a lingering
warmth remained in it. To call this a discovery would perhaps be exaggerating, but it was worth a moment's attention.

He did not feel that he was particularly degenerate. But
he was not at all disposed only to spiritual rape. It was like
eating unsweetened tapioca. Spiritual rape meant that before he could hurt her, he would have to hurt himself. And
why should he contract even a psychological venereal dis-

ease? That would be adding insult to injury. Was it true that a woman's glands were so weak that they emitted blood just because a man looked at her?

He vaguely sensed that there were two kinds of sexual desire. For example, on the basis of the Möbius circle, when you courted a girl, you always began, it seemed, with lectures on nutrition and taste . . . that is, before you got around to sex. Food exists only in an abstract sense for anybody dying of hunger; there isn't any such thing as the taste of Kobe beef or Hiroshima oysters. But once one's belly is full, then one begins to discern differences in taste and textures. Sexual desire was the same. First came desire in general, and only after that did particular sexual tastes evolve. And sex couldn't be discussed in general; it depended on time and place . . . sometimes you needed a dose of vitamins . . . sometimes a bowl of eels and rice. It was a well-thought-out theory, but regrettably not a single girl friend had offered herself to him in support of it, with a readiness to experience sexual desire in general or sex in particular. That was natural. No man or woman is wooed by theory alone. He knew this, but he naïvely observed the theory of the Möbius circle and kept repeatedly pushing the doorbell of an empty house, only because he did not want to commit spiritual rape.

To be sure, he himself wasn't so romantic as to dream of pure sexual relations. You could do that when you were looking death in the eye . . . like the bamboo grass that bears seeds just as it is beginning to wither . . . like starving mice that repeatedly and frantically copulate as they migrate . . . like tuberculosis patients who are all seized by a kind of sex madness . . . like the king or ruler who dwells in a tower and devotes himself to establishing a harem . . . like the soldier for whom every moment is precious as he awaits the enemy attack and who spends those final moments masturbating. . . .

Fortunately, however, man is not indiscriminately exposed to the dangers of death. Man no longer needs to fear, even in winter; he has been able to free himself of the seasonal sexual urge. Yet when the struggle is over, weapons become an encumbrance. Order has come about, and the power to control sex and brute force lies within man's grasp, in place of Nature's. Thus, sexual intercourse is like a commutation ticket: it has to be punched every time you use it. Of course, you must check to see that the ticket is genuine. But this checking is terribly onerous; it corresponds precisely to the complications of order. All kinds of certificates—contracts, licenses, I.D. cards, permits, certificates of title, authorizations, registrations, carrying permits, certificates of membership, letters of recommendation, notes, leases, temporary permits, agreements, income declarations, receipts, even certificates of ancestry . . . every conceivable type of paper must be mobilized into action.

Thanks to such checks, sex is completely buried under a mantle of certifications . . . like a basket worm. It would be all right, I suppose, if this were satisfying. But even so, would that be the end of certificates? Wouldn't there be something else we had forgotten to declare? Both men and women are captives of an oppressive jealousy, always suspicious that the other party has purposely left something out. To demonstrate their honesty they are compelled to issue a new certificate. No one knows where it will ever stop. In the last analysis, the certificate seems to be infinite.

(She blames me for being too argumentative. But I'm not the one who's argumentative. It's just the truth.)

"But isn't that the obligation of love?"

"Not at all. It's what's left after you have struck out the restrictions by a process of elimination. If you don't have that much confidence, you might just as well not have any at all."

There's no obligation to go along with this to the extent —and the poor taste—of gift-wrapping sex. Let's be freshly pressed every morning in sex too. In sex, once the coat's been worn, it's already old. You press out the wrinkles and it's like new again. Once it's new, it's immediately old again. . . . Is there any obligation to listen to such indecencies?

Of course, if he could feel that this regularization offered some guarantee for life, then there was still room for compromise. But what about reality? The thorn of death falls from heaven, and its myriad forms leave us no room to move. In sex, too, one seems to have a vague premonition, a feeling that one has been left with a false promissory note. And so one begins to falsify the commutation ticket because one is sexually unsatisfied. Well, that's all right; it's good business. Or one admits of spiritual rape as a necessary evil. Anyway, without it there would be almost no marriages. Those who are in favor of free sex behave in much the same way. They are only giving a plausible rationalization to mutual rape. If you accept it as such, it can be enjoyed too. Freedom combined with constant worry—

like a curtain that does not quite close—can only result in sexual psychopaths. There was no opportunity for his pitiable sex to doff its hat and relax.

The woman seemed to sense the workings of the man's emotions. She stopped in the midst of tying the string to her trousers, and the end of the loosened thong hung down from between her hands. She looked up at him with rabbit-like eyes. And it was not only because of their red eyelids that they resembled a rabbit's. The man answered her with eyes in which time had ceased to run. A strong smell like boiled gristle surrounded her.

Still grasping the thong, she slipped by him and went up to her room, where she began to take off her trousers. Her manner was so completely natural that she seemed to be continuing what she had been doing before. The man inwardly rubbed his hands in expectation: such a woman was a real woman. But he immediately reconsidered. Stupid! With such hesitancy he would surely botch the thing. Hastily he too put his hand to his belt. If this had been yesterday he would have perhaps assumed her behavior to be a woman's transparent play-acting . . . like her giggles and dimples. Actually that might be the case. But he did not want to think so. The stage at which he could bargain for her body had long passed. Now, force had decided the situation. There was ample basis for thinking that relations would be mutually agreeable, and bargaining for permission could be dismissed.

A little flow of sand, along with his trousers, slid over the base of his member and fell along his thighs. A stench like

that of musty socks rose up. Slowly, but surely, with a
pumping like that of a water pipe in which the water has
been turned off, his member began to fill again. Hatless, his
penis indicating the direction, he spread his wings and
melted in behind the already naked woman.

Would he find it enjoyable? Of course everything fitted,
as if into a square of equally spaced graph paper: breathing, time, the room, the woman. Was this what the Möbius
man called general sexual desire? Maybe, but what tight buttocks! You couldn't compare them to the frustrated bags
of bones you picked up in the streets.

The woman, sitting on one knee, had begun to brush
the sand from her neck with a towel which she had
rolled into a ball. Suddenly there was an avalanche of sand.
The whole house trembled and groaned. A provoking inter-
ference! Before his very eyes, a mistlike sand covered the
woman's head with white, collecting on her shoulders and
arms. The two, clutched in each other's arms, could only
wait for the avalanche to pass.

Their sweat trickled onto the sand which had gathered,
and on that still more sand fell. The woman's shoulders
trembled. He felt like superheated water, as if he were on
the verge of boiling over. Yet he could not understand why
he was so terribly attracted by her thighs. But he was . . .
so much that he felt like taking the nerves of his body and
coiling them one by one around them. The appetite of
meat-eating animals must be just this—coarse, voracious.
He fought back like a coiled spring. This was an experience
he had not had with the other. On that bed—with the other
one—they had been a feeling man and woman, a watching

man and woman; they had been a man who watched himself experiencing and a woman who watched herself experiencing; they had been a woman who watched a man watching himself and a man watching a woman watching herself . . . all reflected in counter-mirrors . . . the limitless consciousness of the sexual act. Sexual desire, with a history of some hundred million years from the amoeba on up, is fortunately not easily worn out. But what he needed now was a voracious passion, a stimulation that would sweep his nerves into the woman's loins.

The sand avalanche stopped, and as though he had been waiting for it to do so, he joined the woman in helping to brush the sand from her body. She laughed in a husky voice. His hands became more and more insistent as they passed from her breasts under her arms and from there around her loins. Her fingers dug into his neck, and now and then she would give little cries of surprise.

When he had finished, it was her turn to brush his body. He closed his eyes and waited, passing his hand over her hair, which was hard and rough to the touch.

There was a spasmodic contraction, and again the same thing . . . the same changeless repetition to which he had devoted himself, dreaming of other things: eating, walking, sleeping, hiccoughing, bawling, copulating.

21

~~~~~~~~~~~~~~~~~~~~~~

MAN's convulsions go on building endless layers of fossils.
Dinosaur teeth and glaciers were powerless against this re-
productive drive with its screams and its ecstasy. Finally a
white flash squeezed his writhing body dry . . . a meteoric
swarm spurted out, piercing the limitless darkness . . .
rusty, orange-colored stars . . . an alkaline chorus.

The glimmer trailed on and disappeared at last. The
woman's hands patting him on the buttocks to urge him on
no longer had any effect. His nerves, which had streamed
into her, had withered back like a frost-bitten radish, and
his member was paralyzed between the lips of the conch.
The woman, who had thrust out her hips, reluctant to let
him go, also sank back exhausted in a breathless contentment.

An old rag rankly sour behind a chest of drawers . . .
an avenue in front of a bicycle track, from which he used
to return covered with the dust of regret.

In the final analysis, nothing had been of any avail,
nothing had been finished. It was not he who had satisfied
his desires, but apparently someone quite different, someone who had borrowed his body. Sex, of its nature, was not
defined by a single, individual body but by the species. An
individual, finished with his squalid act, must return at

once to his former self. Only the happy ones return to contentment. Those who were sad return to despair. Those who were dying return to their deathbeds. How could he possibly be convinced that such trickery was passionate love? Was there anything better in this passionate love than in commutation sex? If there were, it would be better to be some ascetic made of glass. Apparently he had dozed off for a moment, rolling over in the sweat and secretions which smelled like rancid fish oil. He had dreamed. It was a dream about a lavatory which he could never find although he could hear the sound of water, about a common bathroom where the toilet was filled to overflowing with feces, about a long gallery whose flooring was beginning to warp, about a cracked glass. There was a man, running with a canteen. When he asked him for just a swallow of water, the man scowled at him, making a face like a grasshopper, and rushed off.

He awoke. A hot, sticky glue was melting on the back of his tongue. His thirst had returned twofold. He wanted water. Sparkling, crystalline water, with silver spurs of air bubbles rising from the bottom of the glass. He was an empty water pipe in a deserted house, covered with spider webs and smeared with dust, gasping like a fish.

When he stood up, his hands and feet felt like heavy rubber bags of water. He picked up the empty kettle, which had been thrown on the earthen floor, and tipped it to his mouth. After more than thirty seconds, two, three drops finally dampened the end of his tongue. But it remained as dry as blotting paper. His expectant throat convulsed even more, as if it had gone insane.

Frantic for water, he rummaged around in the vicinity of the sink for anything he could get his hands on. Of all chemical compounds water was the simplest one. It should not be impossible to find some somewhere . . . like a penny forgotten in a desk drawer. There! He smelled water. Without a doubt it was the smell of water. He hastily scraped some wet sand from the bottom of the water jar and stuffed his mouth full. A feeling of nausea welled up in him. He bent over, his stomach convulsed, and his tears began to flow as he vomited up a yellow gastric liquid.

The pain of his headache slipped down over his eyes like a leaden visor. Apparently passion was simply a short-cut to collapse. Suddenly he rose to his hands and knees, and like a dog began to dig in the sand of the earthen floor. When he had dug to the depth of his elbows, the sand was dark and moist. He thrust his face into it, pressed his burning forehead against it, inhaling it deeply. The oxygen and hydrogen might conceivably combine.

"Goddamn dirty hands!" he snapped, pressing his nails into the palms of his hands and turning toward the woman. "What in God's name are you going to do? Isn't there really any water any place?"

The woman spoke in a whisper, turning the upper part of her body away, and drawing her kimono over her naked thighs. "No. There's not any."

"Not any? Do you think you can let it go at that? This is a matter of life and death! You bitch! Do something! And make it quick. Please! See, I'm even saying please!"

"Well, if we just got down to work . . . in no time at all they'd . . ."

"All right. You win. I can't help it. I give in." In his heart he had not given in for a minute. But this was certainly no way to die . . . he was not a dried sardine, after all. Yet he would have made a fool of himself for anyone to see if only he could get hold of some water.

"I really give in. But it's pretty bad to make us wait until

the regular delivery. We can't very well work when we're this dried out, can we? Get in touch with them right away . . . please. Aren't you thirsty too?"

"They'll know the minute we begin to work. There's always someone watching with binoculars from the fire tower."

"The fire tower . . what fire tower?"

More than iron doors, more than walls, it is the tiny peephole that really makes the prisoner feel locked in. Distressed, the man hastily went back through his memories of the village.

He remembered the horizon of sand and sky. There was no place for a fire tower to be. Moreover, he could not believe that he and the woman could be seen from the outside while they could see no one from where they were.

"You'll understand if you'll take a look by the edge of the cliff out back."

He meekly bent down and picked up the shovel. To worry about his self-respect after all that happened would be like ironing a grimy shirt. He went out as if driven.

The sand was burning like an empty pot over a fire. The glare took his breath away. The air that filled his nostrils smelled of soap. But with each step he was getting that much closer to water. When he stood under the cliff on the sea side and looked up, he could make out the top of a black tower about the size of the tip of his little finger. The thornlike projection was doubtless a lookout. Had he already been noticed? The lookout had doubtless been waiting gloatingly for this moment.

He turned toward the black thorn and, holding the

shovel over his head, waved it furiously back and forth. He adjusted the angle of the blade so that it would reflect into the eyes of the watcher. A film of burning quicksilver spread over his eyes. Whatever was the woman doing? She had better come and help right away.

Suddenly a cool shadow fell over him like a damp hand-kerchief: a cloud had crossed above, like some fallen leaf driven before the wind into a corner of the sky. Damn it . . . if it would only rain he would not have to do this. He would hold out his two hands and they would be filled with water. Streams of water on the windowpanes . . . pillars of water bursting from the eaves troughs . . . splashing rain veiling the asphalt.

He did not know whether he was dreaming or whether his musings had become real, but suddenly he was aware of a commotion around him. Coming to himself, he found that he was in the midst of a sand slide. He took shelter under the eaves of the house and leaned against the wall. His bones seemed to have melted like those of some canned fish. His thirst burst around his temples, leaving fragments lying scattered on the surface of his conscious-ness like dots standing out in relief. He gritted his teeth and held his hands over his stomach; at last he contained his rising nausea.

The sound of the woman's voice came to him. She was facing the cliff and hailing someone. He looked up, squint-ing between his heavy eyelids. The old man who had first brought him here was just letting down a bucket, sus-pended at the end of a rope. Water! At last it had come! The bucket tipped and made a splotch on the sandy slope.

It was water, unmistakably the real thing! With a shout he fairly flew through the air to get to it.

When he came within reach of the bucket he pushed the woman aside, trampling her with his feet, and took hold of it with both hands. He could hardly take off the rope before he impatiently thrust his face into the bucket, his body heaving like a pump. He raised his face and took a breath. The third time he rasied his head water spurted from his nose and his lips, and he choked painfully. His knees buckled limply under him and he closed his eyes. Now it was the woman's turn. She was not to be outdone, and, sounding as if her whole body had turned into a rubber plunger, in no time at all she had drained half the contents.

Then she let go of the bucket and went back to the earthen floor; the old fellow began to haul in the rope. At once the man jumped up and grabbed it. "Wait!" he appealed. "Just a minute. I want you to listen to me. Wait, please! I just want you to listen to me!"

The old man gave in, and his hands stopped moving. He blinked his eyes in a puzzled way, but he remained almost expressionless.

"Since you've given me water, I'll do what I'm supposed to. I promise you that. But I still would like you to listen to me. You have really quite misjudged things. I'm a teacher in a school. I have my colleagues and the union waiting there, and the Board of Education and the P.T.A. too. Do you think people will accept my disappearance in silence?"

The old man ran his tongue over his upper lip and

grinned rather indifferently. It really wasn't a grin, but probably only wrinkles in the corner of his eyes as he tried to keep out the sand that was blown along with the wind. But not a single wrinkle escaped the desperate man's notice.

"What? What's that? You realize, don't you, that you're pretty close to a criminal offense?"

"Why? It's been ten days, but there's been no notice from the local police." The old man repeated his words

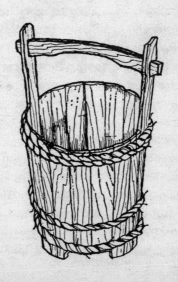

meticulously one by one. "Supposing there was no notice even after ten days . . . what then?"

"It hasn't been ten days. A week!"

The old man shut his mouth and said nothing more. Certainly the exchange of words had been to no purpose. He restrained his impatience and said in a tight voice: "Well, these are matters of little consequence. Won't you come down so we can sit and have a leisurely talk? I will do absolutely nothing out of the way. Even if I wanted to, I couldn't do a thing against such odds. I promise."

The old fellow remained silent. The man began to breathe harder. "It's not that I don't understand how important this work of clearing away the sand is for the village. It's a matter of life and death, I know. It's very serious. I really understand that. If I weren't forced into it, I might even feel like co-operating with you voluntarily. It's really true. It'd only be human to co-operate when I see how things really are, wouldn't it? Do you really think this is the only way to make me work with you? I doubt it. Haven't you been able to think of a better one? The right man in the right place. If you don't put a man in the right place, you destroy the desire to co-operate. That's true, isn't it? Wasn't there a better way of making use of me without taking such a dangerous risk?" Had the old man heard or not? He turned his head blankly and made a movement as if he were shaking off a playful kitten. Was he perhaps nervous about the lookout in the fire tower? Would it be bad if they were to be seen talking together? he wondered.

"You agree, don't you? It really is important to clear

away the sand. But that's a means, not a goal. Your goal is to protect your life from the sand, isn't it? It is, isn't it? Fortunately I've done some research on sand; I'm especially interested in it. That's why I made it a point to come to a place like this. Sand has a strange fascination for people today. There's a way of taking advantage of this. The place can be developed as a new sight-seeing spot, for example. You take advantage of the sand, you follow it, you don't run against it. In short, you've got to try to make a complete change in your thinking."

The old man opened his eyes. "In any sight-seeing place," he answered indifferently, "there's got to be a hot spring around. Besides, everybody knows that the only ones who make anything out of tourists are the merchants or outsiders."

Perhaps it was his imagination, but the man had the feeling of being laughed at; and he suddenly recalled the woman's story about the postcard salesman who, after meeting the same fate as he, had taken sick and died.

"Well, that's just one example of what you might do, of course. You can assume also that there are special crops suited to the particular properties of sand, can't you? In short, you don't have to stick so unreasonably to the old way of life."

"But we've made all kinds of studies. We've tried raising peanuts and bulbs and things like that. I'd just like to show you how tulips grow here."

"Well, what about breastworks to protect you against the sand? . . . a full-scale breastwork against the sand? I've got a friend on a newspaper, you know. It's very possible to use the paper to start public opinion moving in your favor."

"No matter how much sympathy we get from the rest of the world it won't make any difference unless we get the necessary funds."

"Well, then. You've got to start a movement to get them."

"Maybe, but according to government regulations, damage from wind-blown sand doesn't seem to be recognized under disaster compensation."

"You should work to have it recognized!"

"What can you do about it in such a poor prefecture as this one? We're completely disgusted. Anyway, our present way is the cheapest. If we let the government office have their way we'd be lost in the sand while they're fiddling with their abacuses."

"But I have my own situation to think about!" he cried out at the top of his voice. "You're the parents of children, aren't you? You surely understand the obligations of a teacher!"

At that very instant the old fellow drew up the rope. Taken by surprise, the man released it inadvertently. What impertinence! Had the old man been pretending to listen to what he was saying only in order to seize the opportunity of hauling up the rope? He was amazed when his outstretched hands met thin air.

"You behave like madmen. You've lost your senses. Even a monkey could shovel up the sand if it just had a little practice. I should be able to do a lot more than that. A man has the obligation to make full use of the abilities he has."

"Well, maybe, but . . ." The old man spoke casually as if to put an end to the chitchat. "Do what you can anyway. We'll do whatever we can to help you."

"Wait! Don't joke! Hey, there! Wait a minute! You'll be sorry. You don't understand at all. If you'd just wait a minute. Please!"

But the old man did not look around again. He stood up, his shoulders bent as though he carried a heavy burden, and walked away. After three steps his shoulders were no longer visible, and with the fourth he had completely disappeared from view. The man wearily approached the sand cliff. He sank his arms and head into the sand, which ran in at his collar, forming a loose cushion at the point the shirt met his trousers. Suddenly the perspiration began to pour out furiously from his chest, neck, and forehead and along the insides of his thighs. It was the water he had just drunk! The sand, combined with the perspiration, formed a mustard plaster that made his skin smart and tingle, swelling it into a rubber raincoat.

The woman had already begun to work. Suddenly he was seized by a profound suspicion that she had finished drinking what was left of the water. He hurried back to the house.

The water was all there. Once more he gulped down three or four mouthfuls, and again was amazed at the limpid, mineral taste; he could not conceal his uneasiness. He couldn't possibly wait until evening. Of course, it would be impossible to prepare supper if he drank all the water now. The villagers had counted precisely on this. They intended to get around him by subjecting him to the fear of thirst.

He pulled his straw sun hat far down over his eyes and hastened outside. His judgment and ability to think were no more than a snowflake on his feverish brow when he was faced with the threat of thirst. Ten buckets of water would have been candy, but a single one was merely a goad.

"Where's that shovel?"

The woman smiled wearily, pointing to a spot under the eaves as she wiped the perspiration from her forehead with her sleeve. Although she had been overpowered, she did not appear for a moment to have forgotten the arrangement of the tools. It must be a mental attitude that people who lived in the sands learned naturally.

No sooner did he have the shovel in his hands than his exhausted limbs collapsed like a folding tripod. As a matter of fact, he had not slept a wink since the night before. Under any circumstances, it would probably be necessary to arrange in advance with the woman the minimal amount of work that had to be done. But he was already too tired to talk with her about it. His vocal cords were shredded like strands of dried squid—perhaps because he had strained them too much talking with the old man. Mechanically he took his place next to the woman and began to shovel.

The two, as if bound together, moved on with their digging between the cliff and the building. The board wall of the house was as soft as a rice cake that has not fully dried; it looked like a seedbed for mushrooms. Finally they piled the sand up in one place. They put it into the kerosene cans and transferred them to the clearing. When they had finished, they resumed the digging.

The man's movements were almost automatic, involuntary. A frothy saliva that tasted like egg white filled his mouth. It ran over his chin and dribbled down on his chest, but he paid no attention.

"You know, you would do better to hold the shovel with your left hand further down . . . like this," the woman remarked quietly. "If you hold your left hand still and use the right like a lever you won't get half so tired."

A crow cawed. Suddenly the light changed from yellow to blue, and the pain, which had become magnified, softly withdrew into the surrounding landscape. Four crows glided low, parallel with the coast. The tips of their outspread wings glittered dark green, and the man for some reason was reminded of the potassium cyanide in his insect bottles. Oh, yes. Before he forgot, he must transfer his speciments to another container and wrap them in plastic. They would dissolve into a mushy mess in no time if the dampness got to them.

"Shall we call it a day now?"

The woman looked up at the wall as she spoke. He realized that her face was dry too; she was pale through the layer of sand that clung to her. Suddenly everything around him grew dark, daubed with a rust color, and he realized his blood had lost its vital force. Groping through the tunnel of his dimming consciousness, he barely managed to struggle to his messed and grease-smudged bed. He had no memory of when the woman came in.

22

~~~~~~~~~~~~~~~~~~~~~~~~~~~~

HE would have felt exactly like this if plaster of Paris had been poured between his muscles. His eyes were wide open, but why was it so dark? he wondered. Somewhere a mouse seemed to be dragging along the makings of a nest. His throat smarted painfully as though a file had been passed through it. Gas rose in belches from his intestines as if from some cesspool. He wanted a smoke. No, before that, he wanted a drink of water. Water! At once he was drawn back to reality. Then it hadn't been a mouse, but the woman, who had begun working. My God, how long had he been asleep? He tried to get up, but a terrible weight forced him back on the mattress. Remembering, he snatched the towel from his face. From the open doorway a wan, cool moonlight was streaming in, as if through gelatin. Suddenly it was night again.

The kettle, lamp, and bottle of cheap saké stood beside his pillow. He raised himself at once on one elbow and rinsed out his mouth, spitting the water into the sunken fireplace. Slowly, relishing the feeling, he moistened his throat. He felt around the lamp, and his hand touched a soft package and some cigarettes and matches. He lit the lamp and put a match to a cigarette; then cautiously he tried a mouthful of cheap saké. His scattered faculties slowly began to arrange themselves.

The contents of the package consisted of a boxed lunch: three balls of rice mixed with wheat, which were still warm; two skewers of dried sardines; some dry, wrinkled radish pickle; and some boiled vegetable that had a bitter taste. The vegetable seemed to be dried radish leaves. He could eat only one of the skewers of sardines and one rice ball. His stomach felt like a cold rubber glove.

When he stood up, his joints creaked like the wind howling over the zinc roof. Nervously he peered into the water jar. It had been replenished and was brimming full. He dampened the towel and wiped his face. A shiver went through his whole body like a flourescent light. He washed his neck and flanks and shook the sand from between his fingers. Maybe he should be satisfied with creature comforts and let the rest go.

"Shall I fix you some tea?" The woman was standing in the doorway.

"No, thanks. My stomach is too queasy as it is."

"Did you sleep well?"

"You should have got me up when you got up."

The woman bent her head giggling. "Actually, I got up three times during the night and fixed the towel over your face."

She had the coquetry of a three-year-old who has just learned to use an adult's laugh. It was obvious she did not know how best to express her cheerful feelings or her embarrassment. He felt depressed and turned his eyes away.

"Shall I help you with the digging? Or would it be better if I did the carrying?"

"Well. . . . It's about time for the next basket lift to come."

When he actually began working, for some reason he did not resist it as much as he thought he would. What could be the cause of this change? he wondered. Was it the fear that the water would be discontinued? Was it because of his indebtedness to the woman, or something about the character of the work itself? Work seemed something fundamental for man, something which enabled him to endure the aimless flight of time.

Once he had been taken along—when was it?—by the Möbius man to a lecture-meeting. The meeting place was completely surrounded by a low, rusty fence, and within the enclosure the surface of the ground was almost invisible beneath paper refuse, empty boxes, and rags of indiscriminate origin. What had ever put it into the designer's head to place such a fence around the site? Whereupon, as though his thoughts had materialized, a man in a tired suit of clothes appeared, leaning over the iron fence, earnestly trying to scrape it with his fingertips. His Möbius friend had informed him that it was a plain-clothes man. Then on the ceiling of the meeting place there was a huge coffee-colored leaky spot the like of which he had never seen before. In the midst of all this, the lecturer was speaking: "The only way to go beyond work is through work. It is not that work itself is valuable; we surmount work by work. The real value of work lies in the strength of self-denial."

He heard the sharp signal of someone whistling through his fingers. Then there were carefree shouts and people running up, dragging the baskets. As usual, as they drew nearer they became quiet, and the basket was lowered in silence. He could feel that he was under close observation, but it would be of no use now to yell at the cliff. When the specified amount of sand had been safely hoisted the tension relaxed, and even the feel of the air seemed to change. No one said anything, but it seemed that for the moment they had come to an agreement.

He could see a very definite change in the woman's attitude too.

"Let's have a break. I'll bring some tea."

Her voice and her behavior too were more cheerful. She was brimming over with an uncontainable zest. The man felt sated, as if he had eaten too much sugar. As she passed him he brought himself to pat her buttocks from behind. If the voltage is too high the filament burns out. Never had he intended to deceive her like this. Sometime he would tell her the story of the guard who protected the imaginary castle.

There was a castle. No. It wasn't necessarily a castle, it could be anything: a factory, a bank, a gambling house. So the guard could be either a watchman or a bodyguard. Now the guard, always prepared for the enemy attack, never failed in his vigilance. One day the long-expected enemy finally came. This was the moment, and he rang the alarm signal. Strangely enough, however, there was no response from the troops. Needless to say, the enemy easily overpowered the guard in one fell swoop. In his fading consciousness he saw the enemy sweeping like the wind through the gates, over the walls, and into the buildings unhindered by anyone. No, it was the castle, not the enemy, that was really like the wind. The single guard, like a withered tree in the wilderness, had stood guarding an illusion.

He sat down on the shovel and lit a cigarette. The flame caught at last with the third match. His fatigue spread out into a sluggish circle, like India ink dropped in water—it was a jellyfish, a scent bag, a diagram of an atomic nucleus. Some night bird had found a field mouse and was calling to its mate with a weird cry. An uneasy dog bayed deeply. High in the night sky there was a continuous, discordant sound of wind blowing at a different velocity. And on the ground the wind was a knife continually shaving off thin layers of sand. He wiped away the perspiration, blew his nose with his fingers, and brushed the sand from his head. The ripples of sand at his feet suddenly looked like the motionless crests of waves.

Supposing they were sound waves, what kind of music would they give? he wondered. Maybe even a human being could sing such a song . . . if tongs were driven into his nose and slimy blood stopped up his ears . . . if his teeth were broken one by one with hammer blows, and splinters jammed into his urethra . . . if a vulva were cut away and sewn onto his eyelids. It might resemble cruelty, and then again it might be a little different. Suddenly his eyes soared upward like a bird, and he felt as if he were looking down on himself. Certainly he must be the strangest of all . . . he who was musing on the strangeness of things here.

23

~~~~~~~~~~~~~~~~~~~~~~~

Got a one-way ticket to the blues, woo, woo. . . .

IF you want to sing it, sing it. These days people caught in the clutches of the one-way ticket never sing it like that. The soles of those who have only a one-way ticket are so thin that they scream when they step on a pebble. They have had their fill of walking. "The Round-Trip Ticket Blues" is what they want to sing. A one-way ticket is a disjointed life that misses the links between yesterday and today, today and tomorrow. Only the man who obstinately hangs on to a round-trip ticket can hum with real sorrow a song of a one-way ticket. For this very reason he grows desperate lest the return half of his ticket be lost or stolen; he buys stocks, signs up for life insurance, and talks out of different sides of his mouth to his union pals and his superiors. He hums "The One-Way Ticket Blues" with all his might and, choosing a channel at random, turns the television up to full volume in an attempt to drown out the peevish voices of those who have only a one-way ticket and who keep asking for help, voices that come up through the bathtub drain or the toilet hole. It would not be strange at

all if "The Round-Trip Ticket Blues" were the song of
mankind imprisoned.

Whenever he could, he stealthily worked at making a
rope. He tore his extra shirt into pieces, twisted them together, and then joined them to the kimono sash of the
woman's dead husband; altogether his rope was now about
five yards long. When the time came, he would fasten one
end to a pair of rusty shears, which he would prop half
open with a piece of wood. Of course, the rope was still
not long enough. He could almost make the required
length if he tied on the hemp clothesline and the rough
straw rope, stretched over the earthen floor, on which she
had hung some fish and corn to dry.

The idea had come to him rather suddenly. But it was
not necessarily true that only a time-tested plan would be
successful. Such sudden inspiration had sufficient basis in
itself, even though the process of its emergence had been
unconscious. The chances of success were better in spon-
taneous cases than with plans that had been fussed over.

Now the question was: When should he put his plan
into action? He concluded that the best time for escape
would be during the day, while the woman was asleep. But
it would be risky to cross through the village unless it was
dark. He would begin his actions systematically, leaving
the place as long a time as possible before the woman
awoke, hiding out in some convenient place, and waiting
there until the sun had set. He would take advantage of
the darkness before the moon rose, and it probably would

not be too difficult to get out to a main highway where buses ran.

In the meantime, he would use all his skill to get the woman to tell him about the topography and organization of the village. What were the economics of a place like this, which did not have a single fishing boat although it faced the sea? How long had it been in this condition? What was the population? Who cultivated the tulips, and where? What did the children do? Did they go to a school? If he were to gather together his vague memories of that first day when he had arrived, he could make an approximate map, even though it would be based on indirect information.

Ideally nothing could be better than to escape by detouring around the village and not going through it at all, but the west wall was obstructed by a rather steep promontory which, although not very high, seemed to have become a sheer cliff, having been eroded away since early times by the waves. Even though there were footholds which the villagers used when they went to gather firewood, they were obstructed by thickets and hard to locate; and then it would be unfortunate to arouse the woman's suspicions by being over-inquisitive. On the opposite side, to the east, lay a very narrow creek, which was completely surrounded by uninhabited sand dunes rising and falling for more than five miles and which led ultimately right back again to the entrance of the village. In other words, the village was a bag of sand, cut off at the neck by the creek and the sheer cliffs. The margin of safety would seem to be greater if he attacked the center rather than spending precious minutes detouring, thus giving the villagers more time to rally themselves and catch him.

But that did not mean that the problem was solved. For example, there was the lookout in the fire tower. He was also worried that the woman, upon noticing his disappearance, might set up a hue and cry and that the village gates would be closed before he could get out. Perhaps he could condense the two problems into one. The first basket gang usually came with the water and the regular deliveries a good while after the sun had set. If the woman tried to report his disappearance before then, she could certainly get through only to the fire lookout. The question came down to just what he should do about the fire guard.

Fortunately, owing to the sudden fluctuation of temperature in the region, the surface of the land was shrouded in mist for thirty minutes to an hour before sunset. The reason was apparently that the silicic acid in the sand, which had little capacity to retain heat, suddenly released the warmth it had absorbed during the day. From the fire lookout, the whole area lay precisely at the angle of light reflection, and even with a slight mist a thick, milk-white curtain completely obstructed the view. He had made certain of this yesterday, just to be on the safe side. At the foot of the cliff toward the sea, he had tried sending a signal by waving his towel a number of times, but, just as he had anticipated, there had been no response.

It was on the fourth day after he had conceived it that the plan was actually carried out. He had decided on Saturday evening, which was the usual time the bath water was delivered. The preceding night he had determined to get a full night's sleep by pretending to have a cold. For precaution's sake, he had insisted that they fetch him some aspirin. The tablets were discolored, apparently shop-worn from their sojourn in the local emporium. He took two along with some of the cheap saké; the results were immediate. Until the woman returned from her work, he had heard nothing except the sounds of the lift basket being raised and lowered.

The woman, who had not had to work by herself for some time, understandably bore signs of great fatigue. As she busied herself with the preparation of the meal, he chatted idly about all sorts of things . . . the sink, which had been in bad condition for a long time, should be repaired . . . and so on. He could see that she was thinking that his selfishness was a sign that he was putting down roots here, and she dared not register irritation lest she destroy his mood. Now, after work, anyone should feel like taking a bath. The sand that clung to the skin with the night's perspiration was especially annoying. Not only was it the day for the delivery of the bath water, but the woman especially liked to wash him and would surely not put up any objection.

As he was being soaped he pretended to be aroused and pulled at her kimono. He would wash her in return. Caught between confusion and expectancy, she made a gesture of resistance, but it was not clear just what she was resisting. He quickly poured a bucket of warm water over her naked body and without a washcloth began to pass his soapy hands directly over her skin. He started with the earlobes

and shifted down to the jaw, and as he passed over her
shoulders he reached around and with one hand grasped
her breast. She cried out and, sliding down his chest,
crouched level with his stomach. Undoubtedly it was a
posture of expectation. But the man was in no hurry. With
measured cadence, his hands went on with their pains-
taking massaging from one part of her body to another.

The woman's excitement naturally infected him too. He
felt a strange sadness that was different from usual. The
woman was glowing from within now, as if she were being
washed by a wave of fireflies. To disappoint her now
would be like suddenly shooting a freed criminal from behind. And so he reacted with even greater frenzy, spurring
on his awakening senses.

But there is a limit to perverted passion too. The woman,
who had been entreating him at first, manifested obvious
fright at this frenzy. He was seized by a feeling of pros-
tration, as if he had ejaculated. Again he spurred his
courage, forcing himself on by a series of helter-skelter
lewd fantasies, arousing his passion by biting her breasts
and striking her body, which, with the soap, sweat, and
sand, felt like machine oil mixed with iron filings. He had
intended to let this go on for at least two hours. But finally
the woman gritted her teeth and, complaining of pain,
crouched away from him. He mounted her from behind
like a rabbit and finished up within seconds. Then he
threw water over her to wash off the soap; he forced her
to drink a teacupful of the cheap saké along with three
aspirin tablets. She would sleep straight on through without awakening until night . . . and, if things went well,

until she was awakened by the cries from the basket gangs.

In her sleep the woman breathed as if a paper wad had been stuck in her nose. Her respirations were deep and long; he tapped her heel lightly with his foot, but she showed almost no change. She was an old tube squeezed dry of all sex. He fixed the towel, which had almost slipped off her face, and pulled her kimono down around her knees, seeing that it had twisted like a rope around her waist. Fortunately he was completely occupied with the final arrangements of his plan and there was no time for sentimentality. When he had finished working on the device he had contrived with the old shears, it was just about the appointed moment. As he had expected, he felt a kind of lacerating pain as he looked at her for the last time.

A thin light played in a circle about a yard from the upper lip of the hole. It must be between six-thirty and twenty of seven. The time was just right. He forced both arms back with all his strength and turned his neck to and fro, stretching the kinks out of his shoulder muscles.

First he had to climb to the top of the roof. In grappling, the chances of success are greater the closer the angle of elevation is to forty-five degrees. He would have liked to climb up on the roof using the rope, but he was afraid the woman might be awakened by the sound of the shears striking the shingles. He decided to eliminate the testing and to circle around back of the house and climb up on the roof using as footholds the vestiges of a rain shelter that seemed once to have been used as a place for drying clothes.

The squared timbers were thin and half rotten, and they worried him. But what came next was even worse. The flying sand had polished the straight white grain of the roof, making it appear like new. But when he climbed up on it, it was as soft as a soaked cracker. If he were to put his foot through it, he would be in real trouble. He dispersed his weight, crawling slowly forward. Finally he reached the

ridgepole and, straddling it, raised himself on his knees. The top of the roof was already in the shadows, and the faint honey-colored granulations on the west edge of the hole were signs that the mist was gradually beginning to come in. He no longer need concern himself with the lookout in the tower.

He tied the rope into a lasso and, holding it in his right hand about a yard below the shears, swung it in a circle around his head. His target was one of the sandbags that were used instead of a pulley when they raised and lowered the baskets. Since the bags could hold the rope ladder, they must surely be quite firmly buried. Gradually he increased the speed of the revolutions and, taking aim, let fly with the loop. It sailed off in a completely unexpected direction. His idea of casting was wrong. The shears had to fly in a tangent to the circumference of the hole, and so he would have to let go at the very instant the rope was at right angles with the target, or maybe a bare instant before. Yes, that was it! But the next time the shears unfortunately struck the middle of the cliff and fell to the ground. It would seem that the speed of the revolutions and the angle of elevation as he held the rope were not right.

After repeated tries, he managed to establish both the distance and the angle pretty well. But still there was a long way to go before a real strike. He would have been happy at any sign of progress, but still there was no evidence that the margin of error was lessening—indeed, to the contrary, his aim was becoming terribly erratic with fatigue and impatience. Perhaps he had oversimplified. He

felt unreasonably angry and close to tears, as though someone had actually deceived him.

Yet there seemed to be some truth in the law of probability, according to which the chance of success is directly
proportionate to the number of repetitions. With something like the thirtieth try, when in despair he had given
up hope, the rope flew straight over the bags. The inside
of his mouth felt prickly, and even though he kept swal-
lowing, the saliva kept welling up. But it was still too soon
to be pleased with himself. He had simply got hold of
money with which to buy a lottery ticket. He would see
now whether he would win or lose. All his nerves strained
toward the rope as he drew it gently toward him, as if he
were pulling on stars with a strand of spider's web.

It resisted.

At first he could not believe it, but the rope actually
did not move. He tried exerting more pressure. His body
was poised, waiting for the moment of disillusion . . .
was it to be now? . . . or now? But there was no longer
any room for doubt. The hook improvised from the
shears had bitten firmly into the bags. What luck! What
unbelievable luck! From this minute on, things would
really go in his favor. With a giddy heart, he got down
from the roof and walked to where the end of the rope,
now hanging perpendicular, was gently shaving away at the
sand cliff. Ground level was right there . . . so near he
could scarcely believe it. His face was stiff and his lips
trembled. Columbus's egg must have been hard-boiled.
Keep it hot too long, though, and it would spoil.

He grasped the rope and slowly began hoisting himself.

Suddenly it began to stretch as if it were rubber. He was startled, and the perspiration gushed from his pores. Fortunately the stretching stopped after about a foot. He tried bringing all his weight to bear, and this time there seemed to be no further cause for worry. He spit on his hands, fitted the rope between his legs, and began to climb hand over hand. He rose like a toy monkey climbing a toy coconut tree. Perhaps it was his excitement, but the perspiration on his forehead felt strangely cold. In an effort to keep the sand from falling on him, he avoided brushing against it and depended solely on the rope. But he felt uneasy as his body turned round and round in the air. The dead weight of his torso was more than he had anticipated, and his progress was slow. And whatever was this trembling? His arms had begun to jerk in spite of him, and he felt almost as if he were snapping himself like a whip. Perhaps it was a natural reaction, in view of those forty-six horrible days. When he had climbed a yard the hole seemed a hundred yards deep . . . two yards, two hundred yards deep. Gradually, as the depth of the hole increased, he began to be dizzy. He was too tired. He mustn't look down! But there! There was the surface! The surface where, no matter which way he went, he would walk to freedom . . . to the very ends of the earth. When he got to the surface, this endless moment would become a small flower pressed between the pages of his diary . . . poisonous herb or carnivorous plant, it would be no more than a bit of half-transparent colored paper, and as he sipped his tea in the parlor he would hold it up to the light and take pleasure in telling its story.

And now, he hadn't the slightest intention of accusing the woman any more. He could definitely guarantee that if she wasn't exactly a lady she was also not a prostitute. If she needed any backing later he would gladly guarantee it . . . as much as she wanted. She was a stupid creature whose only merit was that she clung to her round-trip ticket . . . like him. But even with the same round-trip ticket, if the point of departure was different, the destination was naturally different too. It would not be particularly strange, in fact, if his return ticket were to be her ticket out.

Even suppose, for the time being, that she had made a mistake . . . after all, a mistake was a mistake.

Don't look down. He mustn't look down!

A mountain climber, a window cleaner on some skyscraper, an electrician atop a television tower, a trapeze artist in a circus, a chimney sweep on a factory smokestack—the instant of his destruction was the instant he looked down.

24

HE had made it!

His fingernails struck the sandbags and, not caring if his hands were stripped of their skin, he frantically scrambled up. There! He was on top! He no longer had to worry about slipping back even if he relaxed his grip. Yet it was impossible for him to straighten his arms and for minutes he remained as he was, clutching the bags tightly to him.

On this day of his liberation, the forty-sixth he had been in the pit, a violent wind was raging. As he began to crawl along, his face and neck were struck by stinging grains of sand. He had not counted on such a savage wind. In the hole he had just felt that the sound of the sea was closer than usual, and right now should be the moment of the evening calm. Yet if it was blowing this much, surely he could not hope for any mist. Maybe the sky had looked muddy only from within the hole. He might well have mistaken the wind-blown sand for mist. Whichever way it was, the situation was delicate.

He looked up nervously. In the fading light the fire tower seemed to be leaning unsteadily to one side. It was surprisingly slight and far away. But as the man in it would be watching him through binoculars, he couldn't count on the distance to be in his favor. He wondered if they had already spotted him. No, if they had, they would have instantly rung the alarm bell.

On a stormy night almost a half year ago, the woman had told him, a bulwark had given way in a hole located on the western outskirts of the village, and the house in it had been half buried. And then it had rained. The water-soaked sand had doubled in weight and crushed the house like a matchbox. Fortunately no one was injured, but the next morning the whole family had tried to run away. In less than five minutes after the alarm was sounded, they could hear the wailing of the old woman being led along the road in back. The family seemed to have had hereditary mental trouble, the woman had added in a convinced tone.

No he could not waste any time. He raised his head resolutely and looked around. Long shadows fell along the hollows and rises of the dunes. The landscape was bathed in a murky reddishness, and the wisps of wind-blown sand streaming out from the shadows were swallowed up one after the other by other shadows. Could he escape detection behind his screen of blowing sand? Looking back over his shoulder to check on the effect of the light reflection, he stared in amazement. The wind-blown sand was not alone responsible for the pall of milky smoke that lay over the landscape, shading the sinking sun with crayon strokes of color. All at once a shredded and shifting mist was steadily rising from the surface of the ground. If it was blown away in one place, it rose in another; swept clear here, it billowed up there. From his experience in the hole, he was well aware that the sand attracted moisture, but he had had no idea that there was this much. It looked like the scene of a fire after the firemen have gone. Of course, it was a thin mist, not very conspicuous in the reflected light, but a good camouflage, enough to conceal him from the eyes of the lookout.

He put on his shoes, which he had thrust into his belt, and stuck the coiled rope into his pocket. With the shears attached, it would be a useful weapon in an emergency. The direction of his flight was toward the west, which was shielded by the refracted light. His first need was to find a place to hide until the sun went down.

Well, let's get going. Keep your back down and run

along where it's low. Don't lose your head now. Keep your eyes peeled and get a move on. There! There's a hollow to hide in over there! What was that suspicious noise? An unlucky sign? Maybe not . . . up, and get going. Not too much to the right. The cliff on the right was so low that he might be seen.

A path had been worn in a straight line from one hole to another by the night basket crews. The right side of the path was a smooth slope with a number of indentations. The rooftops of a second row of houses were barely visible.

They in turn were protected by the line of houses to the sea side. The walls of the holes all along there were low, and the brushwood fence built as protection against the sand seemed to be still of some avail. From the village side of the wall they could apparently go in and out as they pleased. When he raised his head a little he could see all the way to the center of the town. Roofs of tile, zinc, and thatch clustered in black splotches in the center of the undulating terrain, which opened out like a fan before him. There was a straggling grove of pine, and he could see something that looked like a pond. And just to protect this pitiful bit of geography, more than ten households on the sea side had to submit to a life of slavery.

The slave holes were now situated in a line on the left of the road. Here and there were branching paths made by the basket crews, and beyond, threadbare sandbags buried in the sand told where the holes were. It pained him just to look at them. In some places no rope ladders were looped around the bags, but more places had them than not. Not a few of the slaves, he supposed, and already lost all will to escape.

He could easily understand how it was possible to live such a life. There were kitchens, there were stoves with fires burning in them, there were apple crates, in place of desks, piled full of books, there were kitchens, there were sunken hearths, there were lamps, there were stoves with fires burning in them, there were torn shoji, there were sooty ceilings, there were kitchens, there were clocks that were running and clocks that weren't, there were blaring radios and broken radios, there were kitchens and stoves with fires in them. . . . And in the midst of them all were scattered hundred-yen pieces, domestic animals, children, sex, promissory notes, adultery, incense burners, souvenir photos, and . . . It goes on, terrifyingly repetitive. One could not do without repetition in life, like the beating of the heart, but it was also true that the beating of the heart was not all there was to life.

Down, quick! No, it was nothing, just a crow. There was, alas, no chance of catching it and stuffing it, but such things no longer made any difference. The craving for decorations, medals, tattoos, came only when one dreamed unbelievable dreams.

At last he seemed to be coming to the outskirts of the village, and the road lay atop the ridge of sand dunes; the view opened out, and to his left he could see the sea. The wind carried the pungent taste of surf, and his ears and nostrils hummed like a spinning top. The towel he had tied around his neck snapped in the wind and struck his cheek; as he had expected, the mist here seemed to lack the strength to rise. The leaden sea was overlaid with an aluminum sheet, gathered into wrinkles like the skin on boiled milk. The sun, squeezed by clouds that resembled frogs' eggs, seemed to be stalling, unwilling to sink. The horizon was dotted with the motionless silhouettes of black ships, whose size and distance from him he was unable to guess.

Beyond were only the smooth sand dunes, undulating in countless ridges that stretched on to the promontory. Maybe it was dangerous to go on like this. Worried, he turned and looked behind him; fortunately, the fire tower was cut off from view by a slight rise in the sand. As he raised himself on his toes little by little, his eye was caught by a low-lying shack half buried in the slope immediately to his right. Because of the angle, it had not been visible in the shadows. To the leeward was a deep hollow that looked as if it had been scooped out with a spoon.

An ideal place to hide. The texture of the sand was as smooth as the underside of a shell, and there was not a sign of anyone's having been there. But what was he to do about his own footprints? He retraced his steps and found that beyond about thirty yeards they were already completely effaced. Even where he was standing they were caving in, transforming before his very eyes. The wind was good for something.

As he was about to go round to the back of the shack, something dark came slinking out from the inside. It was a reddish dog, thick-set like a pig. He must not frighten it. Go on, get away! But the dog showed no sign of retreating and stood rooted, its eyes fixed on him. One ear was torn, and its small unbecoming eyes made it seem all the more shifty. It sniffed at him. Would it take it into its head to bark? he wondered. Just let it try. He gripped the shears in his pocket. Let it make a sound and he would put a hole in its brains with these! The dog stared back at him defiantly, but in silence, not even growling. Was it a wild dog? It had a seedy, lusterless coat, and its muzzle was covered with scabs. They say it's a dangerous dog that doesn't bark. Damn! He should have brought some food. And speaking of food, he had forgotten to bring along his potassium cyanide. Oh well, let it go. The woman would

probably never find where he had hidden it anyway. He
held out his hand and gave a low whistle to see if he could
get the dog's attention. For an answer, the dog curled its
thin lips, which were the color of smoked herring, and
bared its yellow sand-incrusted fangs. The brute certainly
couldn't have much appetite for him, he mused. It had a
beastly large throat, though. He had better manage to get
him on the first try, but . . .

Abruptly the dog looked away, his scruff went down, and
he ambled lazily off as if nothing had happened. It had
apparently given in to his unbending will. His mental
power was not in bad shape if he could stare a wild dog
down. He let himself slide into the hollow and lay as he
was, against the slope. He was screened from the wind,
and he gave a sigh of relief and contentment. The dog,
staggering under the gusts, disappeared beyond the blowing sand. The fact that a wild dog had made the place its
home was a guarantee that people did not come around.
As long as the dog did not go tale-bearing to the office of
the farm co-op, his safety here seemed assured. In spite of
the sweat that began slowly and steadily to ooze out, he
felt well. How quiet! . . . Quite as if he were enveloped
in gelatin. Although he was clutching a time bomb, set
for moment X, it bothered him no more than the sound
of the balance wheel of his alarm clock. His Möbius
friend would have immediately analyzed the situation,
so:

—My friend, what you're doing is consoling yourself
with the means of your escape and not keeping your eye
on the goal.

And he would have agreed easily:

—Very true. But I wonder if you have to distinguish so precisely between means and end. Wouldn't it be all right to use the definitions as need dictates?

—No, no, that wouldn't do at all. You can't spend time vertically. It's an accepted fact that time really goes horizontally.

—What happens if you try spending it vertically?

—You're a mummy if you do!

He chuckled and took off his shoes. Indeed, time did seem to run horizontally. He could not stand the sand and sweat that had collected between his toes. He took off his shoes and socks and stretched his toes, letting the air in between them. Hmm, why did places where animals live have such an unpleasant smell? Wouldn't it be fine if there were animals that smelled like flowers! No. It was the smell of his own feet. A curious feeling of friendliness welled up in him when he realized this. He recalled that someone had said that there was nothing that tasted so good as one's own ear wax, that it was better than real cheese. Even if it weren't that bad, there were all kinds of fascinating things one never tired of smelling . . . like the stink of a decaying tooth.

The entrance to the house was more than half blocked with sand, and it was almost impossible to see in. Was it the remains of an old well? It would not be so strange if a shack had been built over a well to protect it from the sand. Of course, you could hardly expect to find water in a place like this. . . . He tried to look in, and this time he was enveloped by the real smell of dog. Animal smell is be-

yond philosophy. He remembered a socialist saying that
he liked a Korean's soul but he couldn't stand his smell.
Well then, if time did run horizontally, it had better show
him how fast it could run. . . . Hope and uneasiness . . .
a feeling of release and impatience. He found it most unbearable to be tantalized this way. He put the towel over
his face and lay down on his back. It might be his own
smell, but he was not about to pay it compliments.

Something was crawling fitfully up the instep of his
foot. Its manner of walking could hardly be like that if it
belonged to the beetle family. He decided it must be
some kind of ground bug, for it drew itself along with
difficulty on its six weak legs. He didn't even feel like finding out. Supposing for the time being it did belong to the
beetle family; even, so he still hesitated, wondering
whether he really felt like going after it or not. He was
apparently incapable of a definite decision.

A breeze flipped the towel from his face. Out of the
corner of his eye he could see a ridge of dunes glistening
and golden. A smoothly rising curve cut off the line of
gold and abruptly slipped away into the shadows. There
was something strangely tense in the spatial composition,
and he shuddered with an uncanny loneliness for people.
(Yes, this certainly is a romantic landscape. . . . A setting
like this would be a great attraction for young tourists
these days. Precious, gilt-edged stock it is. . . . I can
guarantee its future development as someone who's ex-
perienced in this profession. But if you're going to develop
it, first you've got to advertise! Even flies won't come if
you don't advertise. The place might just as well not be

here if no one knows about it. It's like having a precious stone and not finding a practical use for it. Well then, what shall we do? I'll put the thing in the hands of a first-rate photographer and have him make me up some good-looking picture postcards. In the old days you used to find a beauty spot and then have your postcards made. But now, it's common sense to have the cards made first . . . and afterwards think up a beautiful place. I have brought along two or three samples, if you'd care to look them over.) The poor postcard salesman had come with the intention of taking the villagers in, but he had been the one to be taken in, and in the end he had got sick and died. But then, he certainly could not imagine that the card man had been particularly eloquent. He had probably been surprisingly sincere in his hopes for the place and had doubtless staked all he had on the business. What in heaven's name was the real essence of this beauty? Was it the precision of nature with its physical laws, or was it nature's mercilessness, ceaselessly resisting man's understanding?

Until yesterday the very thought of this landscape had filled him with nausea. He had actually thought, in a fit of spleen, that the holes were just right for swindlers like picture-postcard vendors.

However, there was no reason to think of the life in the holes and the beauty of the landscape as being opposed to each other. Beautiful scenery need not be sympathetic to man. His own viewpoint in considering the sand to be a rejection of the stationary state was not madness . . . a 1/8-mm. flow . . . a world where existence was a series of states. The beauty of sand, in other words, belonged to death. It was the beauty of death that ran through the magnificence of its ruins and its great power of destruction. No. Just a minute. He would be in a spot if he were criticized for holding on to his round-trip ticket and not letting go of it. You like movies of wild animals and of war because you find that the same old day, following the same old yesterday, is waiting for you as soon as you come out of the movie house . . . you even like the films that stick so close to reality they nearly give you a heart attack. Is anybody really foolish enough to go to the movies with a real gun, loaded with real bullets? Certain kinds of mice that are said to drink their own urine in place of water, or insects that feed on spoiled meat, or nomadic tribes who know only the one-way ticket at best, can adjust their lives to the desert. If from the beginning you always believed that a ticket was only one-way, then you wouldn't have to try so vainly to cling to the sand like an oyster to a rock. But nomads have gone so far as to change their name to "stock breeders," so . . .

Yes, perhaps he should have spoken about this scenery to the woman. Perhaps he should have sung her the song of the sands, which has absolutely no room for a round-trip ticket, even though he might have sung it badly. At best he had given a poor imitation of a gigolo trying to catch a woman by dangling the bait of a different kind of life. But with his face pressed in the sand, he had been like a cat in a paper bag.

The light on the ridge suddenly vanished. The whole landscape sank into darkness before his eyes. Unnoticed, the wind had died down, and now the mist was coming back strongly. That was probably why the sun had set so abruptly.

Well then, let's go!

25

~~~~~~~~~~~~~~~~~~~~

HE would have to escape by passing through the village before the basket gangs began their work. Judging by experience, there should be about an hour left or, to be on the safe side, forty-five minutes. The spit of the promontory, as if embracing the village, gradually curved in toward the land, reaching as far as the inlet on the east side and squeezing the village road into a single lane. There the sheer cliffs of the promontory ended in what seemed to be slightly elevated, washed-out dunes. If he went straight ahead, keeping the mist-shrouded lights of the village on his right, he could expect to come out just about where the cliffs stopped. It would be a little over a mile. And beyond that lay the outskirts of the village. He could not remember any houses, only occasional plots of peanuts here and there. If he could just get across the dunes, then it would probably be safe to walk down the road. At least the road-bed was red clay, and if he were to run with all his might it would take him about fifteen minutes to get to the highway. If he could get that far, then he would have won the game. Buses would be running, and people would be in their right minds.

Thus, according to his calculations, he had thirty minutes to get through the village. What was bad about the sand was that one wasted strength, not because one's feet sank into it but because there was no resistance. Running was most wasteful of all. Walking with long, careful steps would probably be more effective. And yet, the sand compensated for sucking away one's strength by deadening the sound of footsteps. It was good, at least, that he didn't have to worry about his footsteps being heard.

Well, look where you're walking! It didn't really make any difference whether he fell or not, and he frequently would stumble on the little rises and hollows and sink to his knees. That was all right, but if by chance he were to fall into another sand hole, what in heaven's name would he do then?

It was dark, and the sand stretched forever on in irregular undulations. There were waves within waves, and within the small ones there were many still smaller ridges and hollows. The lights of the village, on which he had made his fix, seldom came into his view, for they were screened off by the crests of the endless undulations. When he could not see the lights, he went on by instinct. His mistakes were always appallingly major. Perhaps it was because his feet turned irresistibly toward the higher places, unconsciously seeking the lights.

Ah! Again he had made a mistake! It was more to the left. If he went on like this he would end up by going straight into the village. Although he had crossed over three small hill-like dunes, the lights did not seem to be getting much nearer. It seemed as if he were circling around in the same place. Perspiration ran into his eyes. He paused and took a deep breath.

He wondered whether the woman was awake yet. He also wondered what kind of reaction she would have when she did awake and realize that he was not there. No, she probably wouldn't realize it right away. She would doubtless suppose he was just relieving himself behind the house. Tonight she would be tired. She would be surprised she had slept until it was dark and would probably be barely able to get herself up. Then, finally, she would remember what had happened between them in the morning from the lingering warmth between her legs, still slightly painful and dry. She would smile bashfully as she groped for the lamp.

But anyway, there was no reason for him to feel any obligation or responsibility for her smile. By his disappearance she would lose only a fragment of her life, one that could be easily replaced by a radio or a mirror.

"You're really a great help," she had said. "It's so different from when I was alone. I can take it easy in the mornings, and the work is finished at least two hours sooner. I think I'll ask the village association to give me some kind of extra work to do at home. I'll save the money. And someday, maybe I'll be able to buy a radio or a mirror or something."

(Radio and mirror . . . radio and mirror. . . .) As if all of human life could be expressed in those two things alone. Radios and mirrors do have a point in common:

both can connect one person with another. Maybe they reflect cravings that touch the core of our existence. All right, when he got home he would buy a radio right away and send it off to her. He would put all the money he had into the best transistor on the market.

But he couldn't promise the mirror so easily. A mirror would go bad here. The quicksilver on the back would peel off in half a year; even the surface of the glass would get cloudy with the constant chafing of the sand in the air. Just like the mirror she had now: you looked in it with one eye, and you couldn't see your nose . . . and if you could see your nose you couldn't see your mouth. No, it didn't matter to him how long it lasted. A mirror was different from a radio; for it to be a means of connection she would first have to have somebody else there to see her. What use would a mirror be to someone who no longer could be seen?

She would be feeling surprised about now. She'd prick up her ears. Wasn't he taking too long about his business? He certainly was . . . the rascal had been clever enough to get away! Would she set up a howl? he wondered. Would she collapse? Or would her eyes just dim with tears? Whatever she did, it was no longer his responsibility. He was the one who had refused to recognize the necessity for a mirror.

—It's a story I read some place. . . . Leaving home is all the fashion now. I thought it was because of bad living conditions, but that doesn't seem to be the only reason. They mentioned a middle-class farm family that had recently added land to its holdings, bought machinery, and was doing quite well, when the eldest son suddenly left home. He was a quiet, hard-working young man, and his parents were completely puzzled; they didn't know why. In country villages you have social obligations and reputation to think of, so there really must have been a reason for the heir of the family to have left home. . . .

—Yes, certainly. An obligation is an obligation.

—Then, it appears that one of the relatives took the trouble to find the young man and hear his story. He wasn't living with a woman, and he didn't seem to be driven by debts or pleasure; there was no single concrete motive. Then whatever was the reason? And what the young man said made absolutely no sense at all. He seemed unable to explain it very well himself, beyond saying he just couldn't stand it any longer.

—There really are foolish people in the world, aren't there!

—But when you think about it, you can understand his feelings. When farmers increase their workable land they have that much more to do. In the final analysis, there's no end to their labor, and they only wind up with more to do. However, the farmer at least has a return on his potatoes and rice. Compared with a farmer's work, shoveling away the sand is like trying to pile up rocks in the River of Hades, where the devils cart them off as fast as you throw them in.

—Well, what happens with the River of Hades in the end?

—Not a thing. It's an infernal punishment precisely because nothing happens.

—Well then, what happened to the son after that?

—He had planned the whole thing in advance and had probably even settled on a job beforehand.

—And then what did he do?

—Well, he went and took his job.

—And after that?

—Well, after that he probably got his pay on payday, and on Sundays I suppose he put on a clean shirt and went to the movies.

—And then . . . ?

—We'll never know unless we put the question to him directly, will we?

—And when he saved up some money, he probably bought himself a radio, didn't he . . . ?

At last, he thought, he had finished his climbing, but he had come only halfway. No, that was wrong. It was already flat here. Where had the lights that he had fixed on gone to? He continued walking with a feeling of disbelief. The place where he stood was apparently the ridge of a rather high dune. Why ever couldn't he see the lights from here? A feeling of apprehension paralyzed his legs. Perhaps his previous laziness was the cause of his failure. He slid down the steep slope, heedless of the direction. It was an unexpectedly long ravine, not only deep but wide too. Many lines of rippling sand lay tangled and confused at the bottom; they troubled his judgment. Even so, he couldn't understand at all why the lights of the village were not visible. His margin of error was not more than a half mile on either side of his line of advance. He may have

missed his way, but it could not be serious. He wanted to
go left, but, perhaps because of his fear of the village, he
also felt he should strike out boldly to the right in order
to get nearer to the lights. Soon the mist would lift and the
stars would come out. The quickest way, in effect, would be
to climb up to any elevated place, regardless of where it was,
and get the best perspective he could.

Still, he couldn't understand. He did not understand at
all the reason why the woman had to be so attached to that
River of Hades. . . . Love of Home and obligation have
meaning only if one stands to lose something by throwing
them away. What in the world did she have to lose?

(Radio and mirror . . . radio and mirror. . . .)

Of course he would send her a radio. But wouldn't it
work out, to the contrary, that she would lose more than
she would gain? For instance, there would be no ceremony
of giving him a bath, which she liked so much. She always
used to save water for washing him, even at the expense of
the laundry. She would splash warm water between his
legs and, quite as if she were doing it to herself, bend over
squealing in laughter. There would not be another chance
for her to laugh like that again.

No, she shouldn't be under any misapprehension. From
the beginning there had been no contract between him
and her, and since there had been no contract there could
be no breach of contract. Furthermore, he too was not
completely untouched. For instance, the stink of the cheap
saké that came once a week and seemed as if it had been
squeezed from a compost heap . . . the flexing of the
flesh on the inner side of her thighs where he could see

the muscles standing out in ridges . . . the sense of shame in scraping away, with a finger he had wet in his mouth, the sand like burnt rubber that had gathered on the dark lips of her vulva. . . . And her bashful smile that had made these things appear more indecent. If he added them all up, they would come to quite a lot. Even if his involvement seemed unbelievable, it was nonetheless a fact. A man, more than a woman, tends to abandon himself to bits and pieces of things.

When he thought about what the villagers had done, he realized that it would be almost impossible to calculate the harm he had suffered. The relationsip between him and the woman was of little importance. He intended sometime to take a full measure of revenge on them. He hadn't yet decided what would be the worst. At first he had thought of setting fire to the whole village, or putting poison in the wells, or laying a trap to lure them one by one into a hole in the sand. He had spurred himself on, whipping up his imagination by thinking up such direct measures. But now that he would have the opportunity of actually putting them into practice, he couldn't continue thinking such childish things. After all, the violence of a single person wouldn't amount to much. The only way was to make his complaint to the authorities. Even if he did, he was somewhat concerned as to how much of the cruel significance of the experience they would grasp. Well, for the time being, he would report it at least to the prefectural police.

Ah yes, and then there was one more thing. . . .

Wait! What was that noise? He could no longer hear it.

Maybe it had been his imagination. By the way, wherever had the lights of the village gone? Even though the land was uneven, it was really too absurd that they were nowhere to be seen. He could easily conceive that he had tended to swing to the left and, having veered too far in the direction of the promontory, was screened from the village by some high ridges. He could waste no time. He would strike out boldly to the right.

. . . Finally, there was one more thing he did not want her to forget . . . she had never been able to answer his question. It had been raining for two days. When it rained, the force of the sand slides increased, but there was much less flying sand. Since they had done a little extra work on the first day of rain, they had been able to take it easy on the next. Taking advantage of the first period of leisure in some time, he had determined to push on tenaciously with a project. He had decided he would try to get at the reason that kept her in the hole, and he would go about it with the same patience one has in picking at a scab left from some skin disease. His perseverance had surprised even himself. At first she had cheerfully let the rain strike on her naked body, but at last she had been driven to the point of tears. Finally she began to say something to the effect that she couldn't leave simply because of the remains of her child and her husband, who had been buried along with the chicken houses on the day of the typhoon. Well, that was understandable. It was quite rational of her, and he could even comprehend her reticence in not speaking to him about it until then. But anyway, he had decided to believe her; he at once determined on the following day to devote some of his sleeping time to looking for the remains.

He had continued digging for two days at the place she had indicated. But he had not found even a trace of the chicken houses, to say nothing of any bones. Then she had pointed out another place. He could not find anything there either. And then she indicated still another. He had dug vainly in this way for nine days, in five different places, and then she had begun to make excuses, looking as if she were about to begin crying again. She had said that the location of the house had evidently changed, shifted by the constant pressure of the sands. Or perhaps it might have been that the hole itself had shifted. She had also said that the chicken houses and the remains of her husband and child might well have been buried under the thick wall of sand that divided her house from her neighbor's, and that they might have moved into the neighbor's garden. It was theoretically possible, certainly. Her unhappy, beaten expression obviously showed that she hadn't meant to lie, but that she had had no intention of telling him from the very beginning. The remains, after all, were no more than an excuse. He had not had the strength to get angry. And then he had decided to leave off trying to figure out who was indebted to whom. She would certainly understand this, he thought, but . . .

What's that? He threw himself headlong to the ground. Everything had happened too quickly; he couldn't grasp the situation. Suddenly the village lay before him. He had apparently been walking straight toward the sandy promontory that was adjacent to it. At the instant the prospect

opened before him he found himself in the very center of
the hamlet. Before he could collect his thoughts, a hostile
barking sounded from a nearby brushwood fence and was
picked up by one dog and then another. In the dark, a circle of white fangs pressed in upon him. He pulled out the
rope with the shears, sprang up, and began to run. There
was no choice. The only thing to do was to make a direct
run for the village gates.

26

~~~~~~~~~~~~~~~~~~~~~~~~~~~~

HE ran.

The houses, floating in the vague light of burning lamps,
formed a maze of obstacles and passageways along the
single path of his flight. He could taste the wind wheezing
through his tightened throat like luke-warm rust. A desperate gamble on a sheet of thin glass that was already bent
to the breaking point. The basket gangs had certainly left
their houses already, but it was still too soon to expect
them to have covered the distance to the seashore. In fact,
he did not remember hearing the sounds of the three-
wheeler. He could not possibly have missed the put-put
of the crazy two-cylinder engine from at least a half mile
away. The situation was extremely serious.

A black lump suddenly sprang out of the shadows. It
was a fairly big dog, judging from its breathing. The dog,

however, had evidently received no training in attack and had committed the blunder of barking just before it was about to sink its teeth in him. He lashed out with his rope, and the shears struck something; the dog let out a baleful howl and melted again into the shadows. Fortunately it had only bitten into the cuff of his trousers. His legs slipped out from under him as he recoiled, and he turned a somersault as he fell. At once he was on his feet again and running.

However, there was not just one dog, but, apparently,

five or six. Discouraged, perhaps, by the failure of the first, the others awaited their chance as they circled around him, barking. Maybe the squat red dog from the shack was urging them on from behind. Then he jumped over a mound of shells in an empty lot and ran between some narrow brushwood fences, cutting through a garden where straw was spread out to dry. At last he came out on a broad road. Only a little more and he would be out of the village.

Just beside the road there was a small ditch. Two children, who looked as if they were brother and sister, scrambled out. He noticed them too late. He did what he could to bring the rope around to the side, but it struck them and all three tumbled into the ditch. Something like a wooden pipe lay at the bottom, and the dull sound of splintering wood accompanied their fall. The children screamed. Damn! Why did they have to yell so loud? He pushed them away with all his strength and clambered out. And at that very instant the beams of three flashlights lined up, blocking his way.

At the same time the alarm bell started to ring. The children were crying . . . the dogs were barking . . . and at every sound of the bell his heart jumped a beat. His pores opened, and a thousand prickly little insects, like grains of rice, came crawling out. One of the flashlights seemed to be of a type that had an adjustable focus, and just when he thought the light was dwindling it suddenly pierced him again like a white-hot needle.

Should he try a frontal attack, kicking them aside as hard as he could? If he could just get across there, he would be outside the village. He might regret the tactic later and then again he might not, but all depended on this instant. Come on! Don't hesitate! If he didn't seize the opportunity now, it would be too late. He couldn't count on a second chance.

Even as he was thinking this, the flashlights, poised in a half circle around him, spread out to the left and the right and slowly approached him. He grasped the rope more firmly and knew he must move, but he only stood there with his toes biting into the soft ground, unable to come to any decision. The places between the flashlights were filled with the dark shadows of men. And that obscure shape by the side of the road, which at first looked like a hole, was certainly the three-wheeler. Even if he were successful in getting through, he would be caught from behind. In back of him he could hear the steps of the children, who had stopped crying, running away. Suddenly a magnificent idea occurred to him: he would get the children and use them as a shield. By taking them hostage he could stop the men from coming nearer. But when he turned to pursue them he could see other lights waiting for him. The road behind had been cut off too!

He recoiled and, gathering his strength, ran back along the way he had just come. His decision was a kind of reflex; he hoped to find some place where he could cut across the dune that lay adjacent to the promontory. The men from the village yelled as they ran after him. His knees felt weak, as if his joints had loosened; perhaps he had been in too much of a hurry. But for the time being, at least, he seemed to have taken them by surprise, and he was able to keep enough distance between him and them in order to turn around now and then to see where they were.

How far had he come? he wondered. He had already run up and down several dunes. Yet the more he strained, the more he seemed to be running vainly, dreamily, in one place. But this was no time to reflect on efficiency. There was a taste of honey mixed with blood on the back of his tongue. He tried to spit it out, but the substance was too viscid. He put his finger in his mouth and scraped at it.

The alarm was still ringing, but it was already faraway and intermittent. The barking of the dogs, too, had become a peevish, distant chatter. It was his own breathing, like a file on metal, that was the disturbance he was aware of now. The three pursuing lights were still in a line, wavering up and down, and while they did not seem to be coming closer, neither did they seem to be getting any further away. It was just as hard for him to run away as it was for them to run after him. From now on it was a question of endurance. But he could not be very optimistic about that. The strain had perhaps lasted too long. His mind suddenly seemed to buckle; in this moment of weakness he even hoped his strength would give out and he would have done with the whole thing. The symptom was dangerous. Yet it was still well that he realized just how dangerous.

His shoes were full of sand, and his toes began to hurt. Looking around, he perceived that his pursuers had fallen back to seven or eight yards behind him, on the right. Why had they gotten off the track like that? Perhaps they had tried too hard to avoid the slopes and had ended up by bungling the chase. Apparently they were pretty tired too. The pursuer, they often say, tires more quickly than the pursued. He paused and hastily took off his shoes, to run barefoot. He stuck them into his belt, since they would be a bother if he put them into his pocket. Recovering his spirits a little, he ran up a fairly steep slope in a single burst of speed. If things went like this and he had a little luck, he might give them the slip yet.

Although the moon had not risen, the countryside was splotched with faint patches of bright and dark from the starlight, and he could clearly distinguish the distant ridges. He seemed to be heading for the end of the promontory. Again he felt the urge to bear to the left. As he was about to change direction, he was suddenly brought up short. If he changed, he would at once shorten the distance between his pursuers and himself. He was thunderstruck, aware for the first time of their plan.

Their pursuit, which at first had seemed implausible, was in fact very well thought out: they were trying to push him in the direction of the sea. Without knowing it, he had been guided. When he thought about it now, he realized that the flashlights were meant precisely to let him know their positions. The way they kept their distance without coming near was certainly done on purpose.

But it was still too soon to give up. He had heard that there was a way to climb up the cliffs somewhere, and if it turned out to be necessary it would not be impossible to swim over to the back of the promontory. He thought of being caught and taken back; there was no room for hesitation. Abrupt descents followed long, gentle rises; abrupt

rises, then long, gentle descents. One foot after another
. . . one step added to the next, like stringing beads . . .
patiently . . . patiently. Unnoticed, the alarm had ceased.
He could no longer distinguish between the sounds of the
wind and sea and the ringing in his ears. He ran up a
hillock and looked around. The pursuers' lights had disappeared. He waited for a moment, but they did not reap-
pear.

Had he really gotten away? he wondered.

His rising hope made his heart beat faster. If it were true,
it was all the more reason he should not relax now . . .
one more dash . . . on to the next rise!

Suddenly it was hard to run. His legs felt strangely
heavy. It was not only the feeling of heaviness: his legs
had actually begun to sink. It was like being in snow, he
thought, and by then he had sunk to his calves. Astonished,
he pulled out one foot and the other sank quickly until he
was knee-deep. What was happening? He had heard of
sand that swallowed people up. He struggled, trying to
extricate himself some way, but the more he struggled,
the more deeply he sank. His two legs were already buried
up to the thighs.

Ah! So this was the trap! Their target had not been the
sea at all, but here! They intended quite simply to liquidate
him without even going to the trouble of capturing him.
Liquidation indeed! Even a sleight-of-hand artist could not
have done it more smoothly with his handkerchief. Another puff of wind and he would be completely gone. Even
the best police dog would be helpless. The bastards didn't
even have to show their faces any more. They hadn't seen

anything or heard anything. A stupid outsider had lost his way by himself and had vanished. They had managed the whole thing without soiling their hands in the slightest.

Sinking . . . sinking . . . soon he would be up to his waist. . . . What in God's name could he do? If he could increase the area of contact with the sand, his body weight per square inch would be lighter, and perhaps he would be able to arrest the sinking somewhat. He flopped down, his arms spread out. However, it was already too late. He had intended to lie on his stomach, but the lower half of his body was now fixed vertically in the sand. It was impossible to keep his already exhausted hips at a right angle for any length of time. Unless one were a trained trapeze artist, sooner or later there would be a limit to this position.

How dark it was. The whole world had closed its eyes and stopped its ears. No one would even turn around to look at his death spasms. Fear convulsed his throat and suddenly burst out. His jaw dropped open, and he gave an animal-like cry.

"Help!"

The stock expression! Well, let it be a stock expression. What was the use of individuality when one was on the point of death? He wanted to go on living under any circumstances, even if his life had no more individuality than a pea in a pod. Soon he would be up to his chest, to his chin, to his nose. . . . Stop! This was enough!

"Help! Please! I'll promise anything! Please! Help! Please!"

At last he began to weep. At first his sobbing remained under control, but soon it changed to unrestrained bawling.

He submitted to his fear with the horrible feeling that all was lost. There was no one to see him, it made no difference. It was too unfair that all this was actually happening without any of the formalities being observed. When a condemned criminal died, he at least left a record. He would yell as much as he wanted. Since no one was there to see . . . he might as well. . . .

And so, when voices called to him suddenly from behind, his surprise was all the more shattering. He was completely defeated. Even his feeling of shame vanished like the shriveled ash of a dragonfly's wing.

"Hey, there! Take hold of this!"

A long piece of board slid down to him and hit his side. A circle of light cut through the darkness and fell on the board. He twisted the disabled upper part of his body, entreating the men he felt were behind him.

"Pull me up with this rope, won't you? . . ."

"No, no. We can't pull you out as if you were a root." A laughing voice broke out behind him. He could not be sure, but there seemed to be four or five of them.

"Just hold on a little longer; we've sent for a shovel. Just put your elbows on that piece of wood and you'll be all right."

He placed his elbows as he was told and cradled his head in his arms. His hair was soaked with perspiration. He felt no particular emotion except that he wanted to have done with this shameful situation as quickly as possible.

"Say, there. . . . You're lucky we followed you. This is a regular mush around here; even the dogs stay away. You really were in danger. . . . Lots of people have wandered in here without knowing it, and they've never come back. The place is a mountain cove; there's a lot of drifting. In winter the snows blow over, and the sand over that, then the snow comes again. This has been going on for about a hundred years until it's become like a pile of thin crackers. At least that's what the old union chief's second boy said, the one who went to school in town. It's interesting, isn't it? If you dig down to the bottom you may find something valuable. . . ."

Whatever was he telling him this for? He could stop talking so innocently any time, as if he didn't know the truth! It would be better if he would just show his colors. Or he would at least prefer to be left alone with his own tattered resignation.

At length there was a commotion behind him. The shovel had evidently arrived. Three men wearing boards attached to the soles of their shoes clumsily began to shovel around him in a wide circle. They stripped the sand away in layers. His dreams, desperation, shame, concern with appearances—all were buried under the sand. And so, he was completely unmoved when their hands touched his shoulders. If they had ordered him to, he would have dropped his trousers and defecated before their very eyes. The sky had grown lighter, and it looked as though the moon would soon rise. How would the woman welcome him back? It really made no difference to him any more. Now, he was nothing more than a punching bag to be knocked around.

27

~~~~~~~~~~~~~~~~~~~~

A ROPE was passed under his arms, and like a piece of baggage, he was again lowered into the hole. No one said a word; it was as if they were at an interment. The hole was deep and dark. The moonlight enveloped the dune landscape in a silken light, making the footprints and the ripples of sand stand out like pleated glass. But the hole, refusing a role in the scenery, was pitch-black. It didn't particularly bother him. He was so exhausted that merely raising his head to look at the moon made him feel dizzy and nauseated.

The woman was a black splotch against the black. She walked with him as he went toward the bed, but for some reason he could not see her at all. No, it was not the woman alone; everything around him was blurred. Even after he had fallen onto the bed, in his mind he was still running with all his might over the sands. Even in his dreaming he continued to run. But his sleep was light. The memory remained of the distant barking of the dogs, and he could hear the coming and going of the baskets. He was aware that the woman had come back from her work once during the night for something to eat and that she had lit the lamp beside his pillow to eat by. He awoke completely

when he got up for a drink of water. But still he did not
have enough energy to go and help her.

Having nothing to do, he lit the lamp again and absent-
mindedly smoked a cigarette; a fat but agile spider began
to circle around the lamp. It would be natural for a moth,
but it was strange that a spider should be drawn by light.
He was on the point of burning it with his cigarette, but
he suddenly held back. It continued to circle around, quite
precisely, within a radius of seven to ten inches, like the
second hand of a watch. Or perhaps it was not a simple
phototropic spider. He was watching it expectantly when a
moth with dark-gray wings, mottled with white and black
crests, came fluttering along. Several times its enormous
shadow was projected on the ceiling as it crashed against
the lamp chimney; then it perched on the metal handle,
motionless. It was a strange moth despite its vulgar ap-
pearance. He touched his cigarette to its body. Its nerve
centers were destroyed, and he flicked the writhing insect
into the path of the spider. At once the expected drama began. Instantly the spider leapt, fixing himself to the still-
living victim. Then it began to circle again, dragging its
now motionless booty with it. It seemed to be smacking
its lips in anticipation of the juicy meal.

He had not known there were spiders like this. How
clever to use the lamp in place of a web. In a web it could
only wait passively, but with the lamp it could engage its
prey. However, a suitable light was the prerequisite of the
method. It was impossible to get such a light naturally. It
would not do to look for a forest fire or wander about under the moon. Could this be a new species of spider, then,

that had developed its instincts by evolving with man? It wasn't a bad hypothesis. But, in that case, how could you explain the attraction of a moth for light? A moth is different from a spider, and lamplight can hardly be thought of as useful in maintaining the species. And yet the point was the same: both phenomena had come about after man-made lights had come into being. The fact that moths did not all go flying off to the moon was irrefutable proof of it. It would be understandable if this were the habit of only one species of moth. But since it was common to moths of about ten thousand varieties, he could only assume that it was an immutable law. This crazy, blind beating of wings caused by man-made light . . . this irrational connection between spiders, moths, and light. If a law appeared without reason, like this, what could one believe in?

He closed his eyes. Spots of light seemed to float before him. When he tried to catch them, they suddenly swirled rapidly and escaped him. They were like the shadows of beetles left on the sand.

He was awakened by the woman's sobbing.

"What are you crying about?"

The woman stood up hastily, trying to hide her embarrassment.

"I'm sorry . . . I was just going to make you some tea. . . ."

Her tearful voice puzzled him. Her back as she bent over, stirring the fire in the hearth, made her seem strangely jittery, and it was some time before he understood the meaning of it. He was slow, as if he were forcing his way through the musty pages of some book. Yet he was able to turn the pages. Suddenly he seemed so miserable that he was sorry for himself.

"I have failed!"

"Yes."

"I have really failed!"

"But there hasn't been a single person who made it . . . not one."

She spoke in an unsteady voice, but there was a certain strength in it, as if she were defending his failure. What pitiful tenderness. It would be too unfair if such tenderness were not rewarded.

"Well, that's too bad. If I had been successful in escaping, I was thinking of sending you a radio."

"A radio?"

"I have been thinking about it for a long time."

"Oh, no . . . you don't have to do that . . . ," the woman said, flustered, as if she were making an excuse. "If I work hard at my side jobs, I'll be able to buy it myself. If I bought it in installments, the down payment would be enough. . . ."

"Well . . . that's right. You could, if you bought it in installments. . . ."

"When the water's hot, shall I wash your back?"

Suddenly a sorrow the color of dawn welled up in him. They might as well lick each other's wounds. But they would lick forever, and the wounds would never heal, and in the end their tongues would be worn away.

"I didn't understand. But life isn't something one can

understand, I suppose. There are all kinds of life, and sometimes the other side of the hill looks greener. What's hard-
est for me is not knowing what living like this will ever
come to. But obviously you can never know, no matter
what sort of life you live. Somehow I can't help but feel it
would be better to have a little more to keep busy with."

"Shall I wash you . . . ?"

She spoke as if she were encouraging him. It was a soft,
moving voice. He slowly began to unbutton his shirt and
trousers. It was as if the sand had filled his whole skin.
(What was the other woman doing now? he wondered.)
What had happened before yesterday seemed like ages ago.

The woman began to rub some soap on a wet cloth.

PART III

〰〰〰〰〰〰〰〰〰〰〰

28

OCTOBER.

During the day the traces of summer, reluctant to depart, still set the sand afire, and their bare feet could not stand it for more than five minutes at a time. But when the sun set, the crack-ridden walls of the room let in the cold night damp, and they had to get on with the work of drying out the wet ashes in the hearth. Because of the change in temperature on windless mornings and evenings, the mist rose like a muddy river.

One day he tried setting a trap to catch crows in the empty space behind the house. He named it "Hope."

The device was exceptionally simple. It made use of the special properties of the sand. He dug a rather deep hole, and in the bottom he buried a wooden bucket. With three sticks the size of matches he propped open a cover slightly smaller than the mouth of the bucket. To each stick he tied a thin thread. The threads ran through a hole in the middle of the lid and were connected to a wire on the outside. To the end of the wire he attached a piece of dried fish as bait. And the whole thing was carefully concealed with sand. From the outside the only thing visible was the bait at the bottom of a sand bowl. As soon as a crow took the bait, the sticks would slip out, the lid would fall down, the sand would slide in, and the crow would be buried alive. He had made two or three trial runs; everything worked perfectly. He could visualize the pitiful figure of the crow swallowed up by the sliding sand, without having had the time even to flap its wings.

And then he would write a letter and fasten it to the crow's leg. Of course, it was all a question of luck. In the first place, the possibility was very slight that, when he released the crow, it would fall into anyone's hands. He would never know where it would fly off to. Usually, the radius of a crow's flight was very limited. The worst risk was that the villagers would notice one crow in the flock with a piece of white paper attached to its legs and learn all about his plans. All his long-suffering patience would have been for nought.

Since he had failed in his escape, he had become extremely cautious. He adjusted himself to the life of the hole, as if it were a kind of hibernation, concentrating his efforts on making the villagers relax their vigilance. Repetition of the same patterns, they say, provides an effective form of protective coloring. If he were to melt into a life of simple repetition, there might possibly come a time when they could be quite unconscious of him.

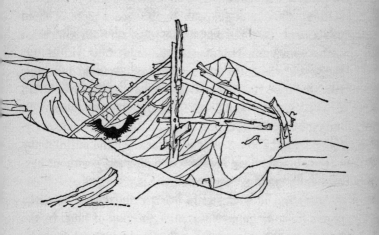

There was another effective element in repetition. For example, the woman had devoted herself for the last two months, day in and day out, to stringing beads, concentrating so fiercely that her face seemed bloated. Her long needle seemed to dance as she picked up with its fine tip the metallic beads scattered in the bottom of a cardboard box. He estimated her savings to be around two thousand yen, enough to make a down payment on a radio in another two weeks.

There was an importance about the dancing needle that made him feel it was the center of the world. Her repetitious movements gave color to the present and a feeling of actuality. The man, not to be outdone, decided to concentrate likewise on some especially monotonous handwork. Sweeping sand from the ceiling, sifting rice, washing —such work had already become his major daily occupations. The time flew by, at least while he was at work. His invention of a small tent made of plastic to shelter them from the sand while they slept, and the device for steaming fish by burying it in hot sand—such things made time pass rather pleasantly.

Since he had come back, in order not to upset himself, he had really tried to get along without reading any newspapers. After a week, he had no longer thought about reading. After a month, he almost forgot there were such things as newspapers. Once he had seen a reproduction of an engraving called "Hell of Loneliness" and had thought it curious. In it a man was floating unsteadily in the air, his eyes wide with fright, and the space around him, far from being empty, was so filled with the semi-transparent shadows of dead persons that he could scarcely move. The dead, each with a different expression, were trying to push one another away, talking ceaselessly to the man. What was this "Hell of Loneliness"? he wondered. Perhaps they had misnamed it, he had thought then, but now he could understand it very well. Loneliness was an unsatisfied thirst for illusion.

And so, one bit one's nails, unable to find contentment in the simple beating of one's heart . . . one smoked, unable to be satisfied with the rhythm of one's brain . . . one had the shakes, unable to find satisfaction in sex alone. Breathing, walking, bowel movements, daily schedules, Sundays coming every seven days, final exams after every four months, far from quieting him, had had the effect rather of pushing him toward a new repetition of them. Soon his cigarette smoking had increased, and he had had terrible nightmares in which he was looking for a hiding place away from the eyes of people with a woman who had dirty fingernails, and when finally he noticed that he was beginning to show toxic symptoms, he suddenly awoke to the heavens governed by an extremely simple elliptic cycle, and the sand dunes ruled by the 1/8-mm. wavelengths.

Even though he felt a certain gentle contentment in the handwork which he performed daily and in the repeated battle with the sand, his reaction was not quite masochistic. He would not find it strange if such a cure really existed.

But one morning, along with the regular deliveries, he was presented with a cartoon magazine. The magazine was nothing in itself. The cover was worn and greasy with fingerprints; it must have been something they had gotten from a junkman. Yet, except for the fact that it was dirty, it was the kind of thoughtfulness the villagers were likely to display. What puzzled him was that he had rolled over in laughter at it, beating the floor and writhing as if he were having convulsions.

The cartoons were exceedingly stupid. They were meaningless, vulgar sketches that had been dashed off, and had he been asked, he would never have been able to explain why they were so amusing. One was so very funny only because of the expression on the face of a horse that had fallen down, its legs broken under the weight of the big bruiser who had mounted it. How could he laugh so when *he* was in such a position? Shame on him! There was a limit to how far he should accommodate himself to his present plight. He had intended this accommodation to be a means, never a goal. It sounded all right to talk of hibernating, but had he changed into a mole and lost all desire to show his face in the sunlight again for the rest of his life?

When he thought about it, he realized there was absolutely no way of knowing when and in what way an opportunity for escape would come. It was possible to conceive of simply becoming accustomed to waiting, with no particular goal in mind, and when his hibernation was at last over, he would be dazzled by the light, unable to come out. Three days a beggar, always a beggar, they say. Such internal rot apparently comes on unexpectedly fast. He was thinking seriously about this, but the moment he recalled the expression on the horse's face he was again seized with moronic laughter. In the lamplight the woman, concentrating as usual on the fine work of stringing beads, raised her head and smiled back at him innocently. He could not bear his own deception, and, tossing the magazine away, he went out.

A milky mist billowed and swirled above the cliff. Spaces of shadow, speckled with the remains of night . . . spaces that sparkled as if with glowing wire . . . spaces flowing with particles of shining vapor. The combination of shadows was filled with fantasies and stirred limitless reveries in him. He would never tire of looking at the sight. Every moment overflowed with new discoveries. Everything was there, actual shapes confounded with fantastic forms he had never seen before.

He turned toward the swirling mass and appealed to it involuntarily.

—Your Honor, I request to be told the substance of the prosecution. I request to be told the reason for my sentence. You see the defendant before you, awaiting your pleasure.

Then a voice he remembered hearing before answered him from the mist. It sounded suddenly muffled, as if it were coming through a telephone.

—One out of every hundred, after all. . . .

—What did you say?

—I am telling you that in Japan schizophrenia occurs at the rate of one out of every hundred persons.

—What in the name of . . .

—Kleptomania also seems to occur in about one out of every hundred.

—What in the name of heaven are you talking about?

—If there is one per cent of homosexuality among men, then naturally there must also be about one per cent of lesbianism among women. Incendiaries account for one per cent; those who tend to be vicious drinkers, for one per cent; mentally retarded, one per cent; sexual maniacs, one per cent; megalomaniacs, one per cent; habitual swindlers, one per cent; frigid women, one per cent; terrorists, one per cent; paranoiacs, one per cent. . . .

—I wish you'd stop talking nonsense.

—Well, listen to me calmly. Acrophobes, heroin addicts, hysterics, homicidal maniacs, syphilitics, morons—suppose there were one per cent of each of these, the total would be twenty per cent. If you could enumerate eighty more abnormalities at this rate—and of course you could—there would be statistical proof that humanity is a hundred per cent abnormal.

—What nonsense! Abnormality would not come into being if there were no standard of normality!

—Come, come. I was just trying to defend you. . . .

—Defend me . . . ?

—Even you will scarcely insist on your own guilt, I imagine.

—No, naturally!

—Then I wish you'd behave more obediently. No matter how exceptional your case is, there's absolutely no cause for worry. Just as people have no obligation to save a strange bird like you, they also don't have the right to judge you either.

—Strange bird? Why does resisting illegal detention make me a strange bird?

—Don't pretend you're so innocent. In Japan, a typical area of high humidity and heat, eighty-seven per cent of annual damage is by water; damage by wind-blown sand, as in your case, would hardly come to a thousandth of one per cent. Ridiculous! It would be like passing special laws against water damage in the Sahara Desert.

—I'm not talking about special laws. I'm talking about the suffering I went through. Illegal detention is illegal, whether it's in a desert or a bog.

—Oh, illegal detention. . . . But there's no end to human greed, don't you see? You're a valuable possession for the villagers. . . .

—Oh, balls! Even *I* have more of a reason for existence than that.

—You're quite sure it's all right to find fault with your beloved sand?

—Fault?

—I hear there are people in the world who, over a period of ten years, have calculated the value of pi to several hundred decimal places. All right, I suppose they have that much reason for existence. But you took the trouble of coming to such a place as this precisely because you rejected such a reason for existence.

—No, that's not true. Even sand has a completely opposite face. You can use it to make casting molds. And it's also an indispensable material for setting concrete. Research is being done on improved farming by taking advantage of the fact that sand easily eliminates weeds and fungus growths. They have even experimented with changing sand into soil by using soil-disintegrating enzymes. You can't talk about sand so sweepingly.

—Come, come, now. What proselytism! If you change your point of view so much I won't know what to believe, will I?

—I don't want to die like a beggar!

—Well, it's six of one and half a dozen of the other, isn't it? The fish you don't catch is always the biggest.

—Damn it, who are you?

But the mist billowed in and erased the other voice. Instead, a hundred sheaves of light, ruler straight, slid down. His head spun, and he smothered a feeling of exhaustion which welled up in him like smoke.

A crow cawed. Suddenly remembering the trap, he decided to go around in back of the house and take a look at "Hope." There was no likelihood of success, but it would be better than the cartoon magazine.

The bait hung just as it was when he had set the trap. The stink of rotten fish struck his nose. It had been over two weeks since he had set "Hope," and nothing whatever had happened. What could the reason possibly be? He had confidence in the construction. If a crow would just take the bait, it would be nabbed. But he was completely helpless, since they paid no attention to it in the first place.

But what could be so displeasing to them about "Hope?" No matter from what angle he looked, he could find nothing suspicious about the trap. Crows were uncommonly cautious because they scavenged for human refuse around where people lived. Well then, it was a question of who would have the most patience . . . until they became completely accustomed to the rotten fish in the hole. Patience itself was not necessarily defeat. Rather, defeat really began when patience was thought to be defeat. He had named the contraption "Hope" originally with this in mind. The Cape of Good Hope was not Gibraltar, but Capetown.

He returned slowly to the house, dragging his feet. It was time to sleep again.

29

When the woman saw him, she blew out the lamp as if she had just remembered and changed her position to a lighter place near the door. Did she still mean to go on working? he wondered. Suddenly he felt an irresistible impulse. Standing in front of her, he struck the box of beads from her knees. Black grains, like grass seed, flew over the earthen floor, sinking at once into the sand. She stared at him with a startled look, but said nothing. All expression suddenly left the man's face. A weak groan came from his sagging lips . . . followed by some yellowish spittle.

"It's pointless. You might as well give up. It's all so pointless. The poison'll soon be in your blood."

She still said nothing. The beads which she had already strung swung feebly back and forth between her fingers, shining like drops of molasses. A slight shaking rose through his body.

"Yes, indeed. Soon it'll be too late. We'll look one day and find that the villagers have disappeared to a man and that we're the only ones left. I know it . . . it's true. This is going to happen soon for sure. It'll already be too late by the time we realize we've been betrayed. What we've done for them up till now will be just a joke to them."

The woman's eyes were fixed on the beads which she held in her hands. She shook her head weakly.

"They couldn't do that. It's not anybody can make a living once he gets out of here."

"It all comes to the same thing then, doesn't it? Anyone who stays here is not living much of a life either."

"But there is the sand. . . ."

"The sand?" The man clamped his teeth together, rolling his head. "What good is sand? Outside of giving you a hard time it doesn't bring in a penny."

"Yes, it does. They sell it."

"You sell it? Who do you sell such stuff to?"

"Well, to construction companies and places like that. They mix it with concrete. . . ."

"Don't joke! It would be a fine mess if you mixed this sand with cement—it's got too much salt in it. In the first place, it's probably against the law or at least against construction regulations. . . ."

"Of course, they sell it secretly. They cut the hauling charges in half too. . . ."

"That's too absurd! Even if half price were free, that won't make it right when buildings and dams start to fall to pieces, will it?"

The woman suddenly interrupted him with accusing eyes. She spoke coldly, looking at his chest, and her attitude was completely different.

"Why should we worry what happens to others?"

He was stunned. The change was complete, as if a mask had dropped over her face. It seemed to be the face of the village, bared to him through her. Until then the village was supposed to be on the side of the executioner. Or maybe they were mindless man-eating plants, or avaricious sea anemones, and he was supposed to be a pitiful victim who happened to be in their clutches. But from the standpoint of the villagers, they themselves were the ones who had been abandoned. Naturally there was no reason why they should be under obligation to the outside world. So if it were he who caused injury, their fangs should accordingly be bared to him. It had never occurred to him to think of his relationship with the village in that light. It was natural that they should be confused and upset. But even if that were the case, and he conceded the point, it would be like throwing away his own justification.

"Well, maybe you don't have to worry about other people," he said, trying desperately to re-establish his position, "but someone is ultimately getting a lot of money out of this sneaky business, isn't he? You don't have to lend your support to people like that. . . ."

"Oh, no. Buying and selling the sand is done by the union."

"I see. But even so, with the amount of investments or stock involved . . ."

"Anybody who was rich enough to have boats or anything got out of here a long time ago. You and I have been treated very well. . . . Really, they weren't unfair to us. If you think I'm lying, get them to show you their records, and you'll see right away. . . ."

The man stood rooted where he was in a vague confusion and malaise. For some reason he felt terribly downhearted. His military map, on which enemy and friendly forces were supposed to be clearly defined, was blurred with unknowns of intermediate colors like indeterminate blobs of ink. When he thought about it, he realized there was no need to get so upset over such an insignificant thing as a cartoon book. There was no one anywhere around who would have cared whether he laughed stupidly or not. His throat tightened, and he began to mutter disconnectedly.

"Well, yes. . . . Yes, of course. It's true about other people's business. . . ."

Then words which he did not expect came by themselves to his lips.

"Let's buy a pot with a plant in it sometime, shall we?" He was astonished himself, but the woman's expression was even more puzzled, and so he could not back down. "It's so dreary not to have anything to rest your eyes on. . . ."

She answered in an uneasy voice: "Shall we have a pine?"

"A pine? I don't like pines. Anything would be better than that—even weeds. There's quite a bit of grass growing out toward the promontory. What do you call that?"

"It's a kind of wheat or dune grass, I suppose. But a tree would be better, wouldn't it?"

"If we get a tree, let's get a maple or a paulownia, with thin branches and large leaves . . . something with leaves that will flutter in the wind."

Ones that flutter . . . clusters of leaves, twisting and fluttering, trying in vain to escape from their branch. . . .

His breath, unrelated to his feeling, sounded shallow. Somehow he felt he was about to break out in tears. Quickly he bent down where the beads had spilled on the earthen floor and began to feel around over the surface of the sand with an awkward groping gesture.

The woman stood up hastily.

"Let it go. I'll do it myself. It'll be easy if I use a sieve."

30

ONE day, as he stood urinating and gazing at the grayish moon, poised on the edge of the hole as if it wanted to be

held in his arms, he was suddenly seized with a terrible
chill. Had he caught a cold? he wondered. No, this chill
seemed to be a different kind. Many times he had experi-
enced the sort of chill that comes just before a fever, but
this was something else. He had no gooseflesh, no sense
of the pricking of the air. It was the marrow of his bones
rather than the surface of his skin that was trembling. And
it was like ripples of water, spreading in slowly widening
circles out from the center. A dull and ceaseless ache
echoed from bone to bone. It was as if a rusty tin can, clat-
tering along in the wind, had gone through his body.

As he stood there, trembling, looking at the moon, a
series of associated ideas occurred to him. The surface of
the moon was like a grainy, powder-covered scar . . .
cheap, dried-out soap . . . a rusty aluminum lunchbox.
Then, as it came into focus, it assumed an unexpected
form: a white skull—the universal symbol for poison . . .
white, powder-covered tablets at the bottom of his insect
bottle . . . an amazing resemblance between the texture
of the moon's surface and that of the efflorescent tablets of
potassium cyanide. He wondered if the bottle were still
hidden under the ledge that ran around the earthen floor,
near the entrance, where he had left it.

His heart began to jump irregularly, like a broken ping-
pong ball. Why did he have to think up such sinister
things? . . . A pretty sad association of ideas. And even
if he hadn't, the October wind carried an oppressive
echo of regret, its reedy voice sounding through empty,
seedless husks. As he looked up at the rim of the hole,
faintly limned in the moonlight, he mused that this sear-

ing feeling of his was perhaps jealousy. Maybe it was a
jealousy of all things that presented a form outside the
hole: streets, trolley cars, traffic signals at intersections, ad-
vertisements on telephone poles, the corpse of a cat, the
drugstore where they sold cigarettes. Just as the sand nib-
bled away at the insides of the wooden walls and the uprights, so his jealousy was gnawing holes in him, making
him like an empty pot on a stove. But the temperature of
an empty pot rises quickly. And it might happen that soon,
unable to stand the heat any longer, he would give up.
First came the problem of weathering this moment, before he could talk about hope.

He wanted lighter air! At least fresh air, unmixed with
his own breath. How wonderful it would be if once a day,
even for a half hour, he could climb up the cliff and look
out over the sea. He should be allowed to do that much.
Their check on him was too strict for him to escape, and
then too it would seem to be a very reasonable request,
considering the faithful work he had performed for them
over more than three months. Even a prisoner in confine-
ment had the right to a period of exercise.

"I really can't stand it! If I keep on like this, sticking
my nose in the sand every day in the year, I'll turn into a
human pickle! I wonder if I could get them to let me walk
around once in a while?"

The woman kept her mouth closed as if annoyed. She
looked like someone who does not know what to do with a
peevish child who has lost his candy.

"I won't let them say I can't!" Suddenly the man became angry. He even mentioned the rope ladder, so hard

for him to talk about because of the loathsome memories. "The other day, when I was running away, I saw it with my own eyes. Some houses in this row actually had rope ladders hanging down to them."

"Yes . . . but . . . ," she said timidly as if apologizing, "most of those people have been living there for generations."

"Well, do you mean that there's no hope for us?"

The woman bent her head with resignation, like a dejected dog. Even if he swallowed the potassium cyanide before her very eyes, she would probably let him go through with it without saying a word.

"All right. I'll try to negotiate directly with them."

However, in his heart he did not expect that such negotiations would be successful. He was quite used to being disappointed. And so, when the old man at once brought back an answer with the second gang of basket hoisters, he was surprised and bewildered.

But his surprise was unimportant compared with the contents of the answer.

"Well, let's see . . . ," the old man said slowly and falteringly, speaking as if he were arranging his old papers in his head. "It's, ah . . . not . . . ah . . . absolutely impossible to arrange. . . . Well, this is just an example, but if the two of you came out front . . . with all of us watching you . . . and if you'd go to it . . . and let us see. . . . Well, what you want is reasonable enough, so we've all decided . . . uh . . . that it's all right. . . ."

"What do you mean, let you see?"

"Well . . . uh . . . the two of you . . . doing it to-gether . . . that's what we mean."

Around him the gang of basket carriers suddenly broke out in a mad laughing. The man stood numbly, as if some-one were strangling him, but slowly he began to understand exactly what they meant. And he began to understand that he understood. Once he had comprehended, their proposal didn't seem particularly surprising.

The beam of a flashlight skimmed by his feet like some golden bird. As if it were a sign, seven or eight more shafts fused into a dish of light and began to creep around the bottom of the hole. Overpowered by the burning, resin-ous ardor of the men at the top of the cliff he was almost caught up in their madness before he could resist.

Slowly he turned toward the woman. She had been wielding her shovel there until a moment ago, and now she had vanished. Had she fled into the house? He looked in at the door and called to her.

"What shall we do?"

The woman's muffled voice came from directly behind the wall. "Let them be!"

"But I want to get out. I really do. . . ."

"But how can you . . . !"

"You mustn't take it so seriously."

"Have you gone out of your mind?" the woman suddenly gasped. "You must have. You've left your senses. I couldn't do a thing like that. I'm not sex-mad."

Was it really true? he wondered. Had he gone out of his mind? He winced from the woman's vehemence, but inside him spread a kind of perverse blankness. He had been trampled this much . . . what difference could appearances make now? If there was something wrong from the standpoint of the one who was being watched, then there was just as much wrong from that of the ones who were watching. There was no need to distinguish between watcher and watched. There might still be some difference between them, but this little ceremony would be enough to make it vanish. And just think what he could get as a prize . . . ground on which he could walk where he wished. He wanted to take a deep breath with his face above the surface of this stagnant water!

Sensing where the woman was, he suddenly threw his whole body upon her. Her cries and the sound of the two of them, entangled, falling against the sand wall, roused an animal-like excitement and frenzy at the top of the cliff. Whistling, clapping . . . obscene, wordless screams. . . . The number of watchers had grown and now included some young women among the men. And the number of flashlights whose light flooded over the doorway had increased at least three times.

He had been successful, perhaps because he had taken her by surprise. Somehow he was able to drag her outside, holding her by the collar. She was a dead, baglike weight. The lights, in a tight semicircle around three sides of the hole, were like the bonfires of some nocturnal festival. Although it was not really that hot, perspiration like a layer of flayed skin poured from his armpits, and his hair was soaked as if he had poured water over it. The cries of the onlookers were like compressed reverberations, filling the sky over his head with great black wings. He felt as if the wings were his own. He could feel the breathless villagers looking down from the top of the cliff, so clearly they could have been himself. They were a part of him, their viscid, drooling saliva was his own desire. In his mind he was the executioner's representative rather than the victim.

The string of her trousers was unexpectedly troublesome. It was dark, and his trembling fingers seemed twice as clumsy as usual. When at last he had torn them off, he grabbed her buttocks in his two hands and shifted his hips under her, but at that instant she twisted her body and wrenched away. He churned through the sand as he tried to catch her, but again he was pushed back with a steel-like resistance. He grabbed her violently, entreating: "Please! Please! I can't really do it anyway . . . just pretend. . . ."

However, there was no need to grasp at her any longer. She had already lost all desire to escape. He heard a noise of cloth tearing, and at the same instant he was struck a terrible blow in the belly by the point of her shoulder, which bore the weight and anger of her whole body. He simply grasped his knees and bent in two. The woman, leaning over him, struck his face again and again with her fists. At first her movements seemed slow, but each blow, delivered as though she were pounding salt, carried weight. Blood gushed from his nose. Sand clung to the blood; his face was a lump of earth.

The excitement at the top of the cliff rapidly folded like an umbrella with broken ribs. Although they tried to join their voices of discontent and laughter and urging into one, they were already out of step and ragged. The obscene and drunken boos and hisses did nothing to arouse enthusiasm. Someone threw something, but he was at once reproved by someone else. The end was as abrupt as the beginning. Cries urging the men back to work trailed in the distance, and the line of lights disappeared as if they had been drawn in. All that remained was the dark north wind, blowing away the last traces of excitement.

But the man, beaten and covered with sand, vaguely thought that everything, after all, had gone as it was written it should. The idea was in a corner of his consciousness, like a sodden undergarment, where only the beating of his heart was painfully clear. The woman's arms, hot as fire, were under his armpits, and the odor of her body was a thorn piercing his nose. He abandoned himself to her hands as if he were a smooth, flat stone in a river bed. It seemed that what remained of him had turned into a liquid and melted into her body.

31

Monotonous weeks of sand and night had gone by.

"Hope," as before, lay neglected by the crows. And the bait of dried fish had become not even that. Although spurned by the crows, it had not been spurned by the bacteria. One morning when he felt the end of the stick, he found that only the skin remained; the fish had turned into a black, almost liquid pulp. As he was changing the bait, he decided at the same time to check on the contraption. He scraped away the sand and opened the cover; he was thunderstruck. Water had collected at the bottom of the bucket. There were only about four inches, but it was more clear by far—indeed it was almost pure—than the water with the metallic film which was delivered to them daily. Had it rained some time recently? he wondered. No. Not for a half month at least. If that were true, then could it be the rain that was left from a half month ago? He would like to think so, but what puzzled him was that he knew the bucket leaked. And when he raised it up, as he had expected, water at once began to fall from the bottom. At that depth there could be no underground spring, and he was obliged to recognize that the escaping water was being constantly replenished from somewhere. At least, that must be theoretically so. But wherever could the replenishment come from in the midst of this parched sand?

He could scarcely contain his gradually rising excitement. There was only one answer he could think of. That was the capillary action of the sand. Because the surface sand had a high specific heat, it was invariably dry, but when you dug down a little the under part was always damp. It must be that the surface evaporation acted as a kind of pump, drawing up the subsurface water. When he thought about it, everything was easily explained—the enormous quantity of mist that came out of the dunes every morning and evening, the abnormal moisture which clung to the pillars and walls, rotting the wood. In short, the dryness of the sand was not due simply to a lack of water, but rather, it would seem, to the fact that the suction caused by capillary attraction never matched the speed of evaporation. In other words, the water was being constantly replenished. But this water circulated at a speed unthinkable in ordinary soil. And it had happened that "Hope" had cut off the circulation some place. Probably the chance placing of the bucket and the crack around the lid had been enough to prevent evaporation of the water that had been sucked up in the bucket. He could not yet explain exactly the placing and its relationship to the other elements, but with study he would surely be able to repeat the experiment. Moreover, it should not be impossible to construct a more efficient device for storing the water.

If he were successful in this experiment he would no longer have to give in to the villagers if they cut off his water. But more important, he had found that the sand was an immense pump. It was just as if he were sitting on a suction pump. He had to sit down for a moment and control his breathing in order to quiet the wild beating of his heart. Of course, there was no need yet to tell anyone about this. It would be his trump card in case of emergency.

But he could not suppress the natural laughter that welled up in him. Even if he were able to keep silent about "Hope," it was hard to conceal the elation in his heart. He suddenly let out a cry and put his arms around the woman's hips from behind as she was getting the bed ready. And when she dodged away he fell over on his back and lay kicking his legs and laughing all the while. It was as if his stomach were being tickled by a paper balloon filled with some special light gas. He felt that the hand he held to his face was floating free in the air.

The woman laughed reluctantly, but it was probably only to be agreeable. He was thinking of the vast network of water veins creeping up through the sand, but the woman, on the contrary, was surely thinking that his actions were sexual advances. That was all right. Only a ship-wrecked person who has just escaped drowning could understand the psychology of someone who breaks out in laughter just because he is able to breathe.

The fact that he was still just as much at the bottom of the hole as ever had not changed, but he felt quite as if he had climbed to the top of a high tower. Perhaps the world had been turned upside down and its projections and depressions reversed. Anyway, he had discovered water in this sand. As long as he had his device the villagers would not be able to interfere with him so easily. No matter how much they cut off his supply, he would be able to get along very well. Again laughter welled up in him at the very thought of the outcry the villagers would make. He was still in the hole, but it seemed as if he were already outside. Turning around, he could see the whole scene. You can't really judge a mosaic if you don't look at it from a distance. If you really get close to it you get lost in detail. You get away from one detail only to get caught in another. Perhaps what he had been seeing up until now was not the sand but grains of sand.

He could say precisely the same thing about the other woman and his former fellow teachers. He had been concerned up until now only with curiously exaggerated details: nostrils in a thick nose, wrinkled lips or smooth, thin lips, spatulate fingers or pointed fingers, flecked eyes, a string of warts under a collarbone, violet veins running over a breast. If he looked very closely at those parts alone he would feel like vomiting. But to eyes with magnifying lenses everything seemed tiny and insectlike. The little ones crawling around over there were his colleagues having a cup of tea in the faculty room. The one in this corner was the other woman, naked, on a dampish bed, her eyes half closed, motionless although the ash of her cigarette was about to fall. Moreover, he felt, without the slightest jealousy, that the little insects were like cookie molds. Cookie molds have only edges and no insides. Even so, there was no need to be such a dedicated cookie maker as to be unable to resist making unneeded cookies just to use the mold. If the chance occurred for him to renew his relationship with them, he would have to start all over again from the very beginning. The change in the sand corresponded to a change in himself. Perhaps, along with the water in the sand, he had found a new self.

Thus, work on a water trap was added to his daily occupations. Figures and diagrams began to accumulate—the place to bury the bucket, the shape of the bucket, the relationship between daylight hours and the rate of water accumulation, the influence of temperature and barometric pressure on the efficiency of the apparatus. But it was incomprehensible to the woman why he could be so enthusiastic about anything so insignificant as a crow trap. She recognized that no man can get along without some sort of plaything, and if he was satisfied with that one, it suited her. Moreover, she did not know why, but he had begun to show more interest in her own craft work. It wasn't at all a disagreeable feeling. The question of the crow trap aside, she had still benefited considerably. But he too had his own reasons and motives. His work on the device was unexpectedly troublesome, for it was necessary to combine many elements. The number of materials increased, but it was hard to find a law that would govern them all. If he wanted to make his data more precise, he needed a radio in order to tune in the weather reports. The radio had become their common objective.

At the beginning of November he had recorded the daily intake of water at one gallon, but after that the quantity began to fall off every day. It was perhaps because of the temperature, and it appeared that he would have to await spring to try a full-scale experiment. The long, hard winter had at last come, and bits of ice were blown along with the sand. In the meantime, in order to get a somewhat better radio, he decided to give the woman a hand with her craft work. One good point was that the inside of the hole was protected from the wind, yet it was unbearable with the sun scarcely visible throughout the day. Even on days when the sand froze over, the amount that blew along in the wind did not decrease, and there was no respite from the work of shoveling. Many times the chilblains on his fingers broke and began to bleed.

In some way, winter passed and spring came. At the beginning of March they got the radio. On the roof they erected a high antenna. The woman joyfully and repeatedly voiced her wonder, turning the dial left and right for half a day. At the end of that month, she found herself pregnant. Two more months went by. Large white birds kept flying over from east to west for three days in succession, and on the following day the lower part of her body was covered with blood and she complained of violent pain. One of the villagers, who was said to have a veterinarian among her relatives, diagnosed it as an extra-uterine pregnancy, and it was decided to take her to the hospital in the city in the three-wheeled truck. The man sat with her as they waited for the truck to come, letting her hold one of his hands, while with the other he kept rubbing her belly.

Finally the three-wheeler stopped at the top of the cliff. A rope ladder was let down for the first time in a half year, and the woman, wrapped in her blankets as in a cocoon, was hauled up by rope. She looked at him beseechingly with eyes almost blinded by tears and mucus, until she could see him no longer. The man looked away as if he did not see her.

Even though she had been taken away, the rope ladder remained as it was. He hesitantly reached out and touched it with his fingertips. After making sure it would not vanish, he slowly began to climb up. The sky was a dirty yellow. His arms and legs felt heavy, as if he had just come out of water. This was the long-awaited rope ladder.

The wind seemed to snatch the breath from his mouth. Circling around the edge of the hole, he climbed to a spot where he could view the sea. The sea too was a dirty yellow. He breathed deeply, but the air only irritated his throat, and it did not taste as he had expected. He turned around. A cloud of sand rose on the outskirts of the village. It was probably the three-wheeler with the woman, he thought. Oh, yes . . . maybe he should have told her the real significance of the trap.

Something moved at the bottom of the hole. It was his own shadow. Just near it stood the water trap. One part of the framework had come loose. Perhaps someone had accidentally stepped on it when they had come to take the woman out. He hastened back down the ladder to repair it. The water, as his calculations had led him to expect, had risen to the fourth mark. The damage did not appear to be too great. In the house, someone was singing in a rasping voice on the radio. He tried to stifle the sobbing that seemed about to burst from him; he plunged his hands into the bucket. The water was piercingly cold. He sank down on his knees and remained inert, his hands still in the water.

There was no particular need to hurry about escaping. On the two-way ticket he held in his hand now, the destination and time of departure were blanks for him to fill in as he wished. In addition, he realized that he was bursting with a desire to talk to someone about the water trap. And if he wanted to talk about it, there wouldn't be better listeners than the villagers. He would end by telling someone—if not today, then tomorrow.

He might as well put off his escape until sometime after that.

NOTIFICATION OF MISSING PERSONS

NAME OF PERSON: *Niki Jumpei*
DATE OF BIRTH: *March 7, 1924*

In view of the fact that a notice of missing person(s) has been filed by Niki Shino (mother), notification of the existence of the missing party should be made to this court by September 21, 1962. In the event of no further report, the said person will be pronounced missing. Anyone knowing anything about the person in question is requested to report to this court by the above date.

February 18, 1962

COURT OF DOMESTIC RELATIONS

JUDGMENT

CLAIMANT: *Niki Shino*
MISSING PERSON: *Niki Jumpei*
DATE OF BIRTH: *March 7, 1924*

A declaration of disappearance concerning the above-mentioned party having been filed, the procedure of public notice having been fulfilled, and the unascertainability of either the existence or the death of the person in question from August 18, 1955, for seven years hence, having been recognized, the following decision has been handed down.

DECISION

Niki Jumpei is hereby declared missing.

October 5, 1962
COURT OF DOMESTIC RELATIONS

SIGNATURE OF JUDGE

A Note About the Author

Kobo Abé was born in Tokyo in 1924 but grew up in Mukden, Manchuria, where his father, a doctor, was on the staff of the medical school. As a young man Mr. Abé was interested in mathematics and insect collecting as well as the works of Poe, Dostoevski, Nietzsche, Heidegger, Jaspers, and Kafka. He received a medical degree from Tokyo University in 1948, but he has never practiced medicine. In that same year he published his first book, *The Road Sign at the End of the Street*. In 1951 he was awarded the most important Japanese literary prize, the Akutagawa, for his novel *The Crime of Mr. S. Karuma*. In 1960 his novel *The Woman in the Dunes* won the Yomiuri Prize for Literature. It was made into a film by Hiroshi Teshigahara in 1963 and won the jury prize at the Cannes Film Festival. It was the first of Mr. Abé's novels to be published in translation in the United States, in 1964. *The Face of Another* (1966) was also made into a film by Mr. Teshigahara. Other novels in translation include *The Ruined Map* (1969), *Friends* (1969), *The Box Man* (1974), and *The Man Who Turned Into a Stick* (1976).

This edition is illustrated by drawings from the pen of Marchi Abé, the author's wife. The Abés live on the outskirts of Tokyo.

A Note About the Translator

E. Dale Saunders, translator of Kobo Abé's *The Woman in the Dunes* (1964), *The Face of Another* (1966), and *The Ruined Map* (1969), received his A.B. from Western Reserve University (1941), his M.A. from Harvard (1948), and his Ph.D. from the University of Paris (1952). He is Professor of Japanese Studies at the University of Pennsylvania, having previously taught at International Christian University, Tokyo, and at Harvard University. Among his publications are *Mudra: A Study of Symbolic Gestures in Japanese Buddhist Sculpture* (1960) and *Buddhism in Japan* (1964).

VINTAGE FICTION, POETRY, AND PLAYS

V-814   **ABE, KOBO** / The Woman in the Dunes
V-2014   **AUDEN, W. H.** / Collected Longer Poems
V-2015   **AUDEN, W. H.** / Collected Shorter Poems 1927-1957
V-102   **AUDEN, W. H.** / Selected Poetry of W. H. Auden
V-601   **AUDEN, W. H. AND PAUL B. TAYLOR (trans.)** / The Elder Edda
V-20   **BABIN, MARIA-THERESA AND STAN STEINER (eds.)** / Borinquen: An Anthology of Puerto-Rican Literature
V-271   **BEDIER, JOSEPH** / Tristan and Iseult
V-523   **BELLAMY, JOE DAVID (ed.)** / Superfiction or The American Story Transformed: An Anthology
V-72   **BERNIKOW, LOUISE (ed.)** / The World Split Open: Four Centuries of Women Poets in England and America 1552-1950
V-321   **BOLT, ROBERT** / A Man for All Seasons
V-21   **BOWEN, ELIZABETH** / The Death of the Heart
V-294   **BRADBURY, RAY** / The Vintage Bradbury
V-670   **BRECHT, BERTOLT (ed. by Ralph Manheim and John Willett)** / Collected Plays, Vol. 1
V-759   **BRECHT, BERTOLT (ed. by Ralph Manheim and John Willett)** / Collected Plays, Vol. 5
V-216   **BRECHT, BERTOLT (ed. by Ralph Manheim and John Willett)** / Collected Plays, Vol. 7
V-819   **BRECHT, BERTOLT (ed. by Ralph Manheim and John Willett)** / Collected Plays, Vol. 9
V-841   **BYNNER, WITTER AND KIANG KANG-HU (eds.)** / The Jade Mountain: A Chinese Anthology
V-207   **CAMUS, ALBERT** / Caligula & Three Other Plays
V-281   **CAMUS, ALBERT** / Exile and the Kingdom
V-223   **CAMUS, ALBERT** / The Fall
V-865   **CAMUS, ALBERT** / A Happy Death: A Novel
V-626   **CAMUS, ALBERT** / Lyrical and Critical Essays
V-75   **CAMUS, ALBERT** / The Myth of Sisyphus and Other Essays
V-258   **CAMUS, ALBERT** / The Plague
V-245   **CAMUS, ALBERT** / The Possessed
V-30   **CAMUS, ALBERT** / The Rebel
V-2   **CAMUS, ALBERT** / The Stranger
V-28   **CATHER, WILLA** / Five Stories
V-705   **CATHER, WILLA** / A Lost Lady
V-200   **CATHER, WILLA** / My Mortal Enemy
V-179   **CATHER, WILLA** / Obscure Destinies
V-252   **CATHER, WILLA** / One of Ours
V-913   **CATHER, WILLA** / The Professor's House
V-434   **CATHER, WILLA** / Sapphira and the Slave Girl
V-680   **CATHER, WILLA** / Shadows on the Rock
V-684   **CATHER, WILLA** / Youth and the Bright Medusa
V-140   **CERF, BENNETT (ed.)** / Famous Ghost Stories
V-203   **CERF, BENNETT (ed.)** / Four Contemporary American Plays
V-127   **CERF, BENNETT (ed.)** / Great Modern Short Stories
V-326   **CERF, CHRISTOPHER (ed.)** / The Vintage Anthology of Science Fantasy

V-293   **CHAUCER, GEOFFREY** / The Canterbury Tales (a prose version in Modern English)
V-142   **CHAUCER, GEOFFREY** / Troilus and Cressida
V-723   **CHERNYSHEVSKY, N. G.** / What Is to Be Done?
V-173   **CONFUCIUS (trans. by Arthur Waley)** / Analects
V-155   **CONRAD, JOSEPH** / Three Great Tales: The Nigger of the Narcissus, Heart of Darkness, Youth
V-10   **CRANE, STEPHEN** / Stories and Tales
V-126   **DANTE, ALIGHIERI** / The Divine Comedy
V-177   **DINESEN, ISAK** / Anecdotes of Destiny
V-431   **DINESEN, ISAK** / Ehrengard
V-752   **DINESEN, ISAK** / Last Tales
V-740   **DINESEN, ISAK** / Out of Africa
V-807   **DINESEN, ISAK** / Seven Gothic Tales
V-62   **DINESEN, ISAK** / Shadows on the Grass
V-205   **DINESEN, ISAK** / Winter's Tales
V-721   **DOSTOYEVSKY, FYODOR** / Crime and Punishment
V-722   **DOSTOYEVSKY, FYODOR** / The Brothers Karamazov
V-780   **FAULKNER, WILLIAM** / Absalom, Absalom!
V-254   **FAULKNER, WILLIAM** / As I Lay Dying
V-884   **FAULKNER, WILLIAM** / Go Down, Moses
V-139   **FAULKNER, WILLIAM** / The Hamlet
V-792   **FAULKNER, WILLIAM** / Intruder in the Dust
V-189   **FAULKNER, WILLIAM** / Light in August
V-282   **FAULKNER, WILLIAM** / The Mansion
V-339   **FAULKNER, WILLIAM** / The Reivers
V-412   **FAULKNER, WILLIAM** / Requiem For A Nun
V-381   **FAULKNER, WILLIAM** / Sanctuary
V-5   **FAULKNER, WILLIAM** / The Sound and the Fury
V-184   **FAULKNER, WILLIAM** / The Town
V-351   **FAULKNER, WILLIAM** / The Unvanquished
V-262   **FAULKNER, WILLIAM** / The Wild Palms
V-149   **FAULKNER, WILLIAM** / Three Famous Short Novels: Spotted Horses, Old Man, The Bear
V-45   **FORD, FORD MADOX** / The Good Soldier
V-7   **FORSTER, E. M.** Howards End
V-40   **FORSTER, E. M.** / The Longest Journey
V-187   **FORSTER, E. M.** / A Room With a View
V-61   **FORSTER, E. M.** / Where Angels Fear to Tread
V-219   **FRISCH, MAX** / I'm Not Stiller
V-842   **GIDE, ANDRE** / The Counterfeiters
V-8   **GIDE, ANDRE** / The Immoralist
V-96   **GIDE, ANDRE** / Lafcadio's Adventures
V-27   **GIDE, ANDRE** / Strait Is the Gate
V-66   **GIDE, ANDRE** / Two Legends: Oedipus and Theseus
V-958   **von GOETHE, JOHANN WOLFGANG (ELIZABETH MAYER, LOUISE BOGAN & W. H. AUDEN, trans.)** / The Sorrows of Young Werther and Novella
V-300   **GRASS, GUNTER** / The Tin Drum
V-425   **GRAVES, ROBERT** / Claudius the God
V-182   **GRAVES, ROBERT** / I, Claudius
V-717   **GUERNEY, B. G. (ed.)** / An Anthology of Russian Literature in the Soviet Period: From Gorki to Pasternak

V-829   **HAMMETT, DASHIELL** / The Big Knockover
V-2013   **HAMMETT, DASHIELL** / The Continental Op
V-827   **HAMMETT, DASHIELL** / The Dain Curse
V-773   **HAMMETT, DASHIELL** / The Glass Key
V-772   **HAMMETT, DASHIELL** / The Maltese Falcon
V-828   **HAMMETT, DASHIELL** / The Red Harvest
V-774   **HAMMETT, DASHIELL** / The Thin Man
V-781   **HAMSUN, KNUT** / Growth of the Soil
V-896   **HATCH, JAMES AND VICTORIA SULLIVAN (eds.)** / Plays by and About Women
V-15   **HAWTHORNE, NATHANIEL** / Short Stories
V-610   **HSU, KAI-YU** / The Chinese Literary Scene: A Writer's Visit to the People's Republic
V-910   **HUGHES, LANGSTON** / Selected Poems of Langston Hughes
V-304   **HUGHES, LANGSTON** / The Ways of White Folks
V-158   **ISHERWOOD, CHRISTOPHER AND W. H. AUDEN** / Two Plays: The Dog Beneath the Skin and The Ascent of F6
V-295   **JEFFERS, ROBINSON** / Selected Poems
V-380   **JOYCE, JAMES** / Ulysses
V-991   **KAFKA, FRANZ** / The Castle
V-484   **KAFKA, FRANZ** / The Trial
V-841   **KANG-HU, KIANG AND WITTER BYNNER** / The Jade Mountain: A Chinese Anthology
V-508   **KOCH, KENNETH** / The Art of Love
V-915   **KOCH, KENNETH** / A Change of Hearts
V-467   **KOCH, KENNETH** / The Red Robbins
V-82   **KOCH, KENNETH** / Wishes, Lies and Dreams
V-134   **LAGERKVIST, PAR** / Barabbas
V-240   **LAGERKVIST, PAR** / The Sibyl
V-776   **LAING, R. D.** / Knots
V-23   **LAWRENCE, D. H.** / The Plumed Serpent
V-71   **LAWRENCE, D. H.** / St. Mawr & The Man Who Died
V-329   **LINDBERGH, ANNE MORROW** / Gift from the Sea
V-822   **LINDBERGH, ANNE MORROW** / The Unicorn and Other Poems
V-479   **MALRAUX, ANDRE** / Man's Fate
V-180   **MANN, THOMAS** / Buddenbrooks
V-3   **MANN, THOMAS** / Death in Venice and Seven Other Stories
V-297   **MANN, THOMAS** / Doctor Faustus
V-497   **MANN, THOMAS** / The Magic Mountain
V-86   **MANN, THOMAS** / The Transposed Heads
V-36   **MANSFIELD, KATHERINE** / Stories
V-137   **MAUGHAM, W. SOMERSET** / Of Human Bondage
V-720   **MIRSKY, D. S.** / A History of Russian Literature: From Its Beginnings to 1900
V-883   **MISHIMA, YUKIO** / Five Modern Nō Plays
V-151   **MOFFAT, MARY JANE AND CHARLOTTE PAINTER** / Revelations: Diaries of Women
V-851   **MORGAN, ROBIN** / Monster
V-926   **MUSTARD, HELEN (trans.)** / Heinrich Heine: Selected Works
V-901   **NEMIROFF, ROBERT (ed.)** / Les Blancs: The Collected Last Plays of Lorraine Hansberry
V-925   **NGUYEN, DU** / The Tale of Kieu

V-125   **OATES, WHITNEY J. AND EUGENE O'NEILL, Jr. (eds.)** / Seven Famous Greek Plays

V-973   **O'HARA, FRANK** / Selected Poems of Frank O'Hara

V-855   **O'NEILL, EUGENE** / Anna Christie, The Emperor Jones, The Hairy Ape

V-18   **O'NEILL, EUGENE** / The Iceman Cometh

V-236   **O'NEILL, EUGENE** / A Moon For the Misbegotten

V-856   **O'NEILL, EUGENE** / Seven Plays of the Sea

V-276   **O'NEILL, EUGENE** / Six Short Plays

V-165   **O'NEILL, EUGENE** / Three Plays: Desire Under the Elms, Strange Interlude, Mourning Becomes Electra

V-125   **O'NEILL, EUGENE, JR. AND WHITNEY J. OATES (eds.)** / Seven Famous Greek Plays

V-151   **PAINTER, CHARLOTTE AND MARY JANE MOFFAT** / Revelations: Diaries of Women

V-907   **PERELMAN, S. J.** / Crazy Like a Fox

V-466   **PLATH, SYLVIA** / The Colossus and Other Poems

V-232   **PRITCHETT, V. S.** / Midnight Oil

V-598   **PROUST, MARCEL** / The Captive

V-597   **PROUST, MARCEL** / Cities of the Plain

V-596   **PROUST, MARCEL** / The Guermantes Way

V-600   **PROUST, MARCEL** / The Past Recaptured

V-594   **PROUST, MARCEL** / Swann's Way

V-599   **PROUST, MARCEL** / The Sweet Cheat Gone

V-595   **PROUST, MARCEL** / Within A Budding Grove

V-714   **PUSHKIN, ALEXANDER** / The Captain's Daughter and Other Stories

V-976   **QUASHA, GEORGE AND JEROME ROTHENBERG (eds.)** / America a Prophecy: A Reading of American Poetry from Pre-Columbian Times to the Present

V-80   **REDDY, T. J.** / Less Than a Score, But A Point: Poems by T. J. Reddy

V-504   **RENAULT, MARY** / The Bull From the Sea

V-653   **RENAULT, MARY** / The Last of the Wine

V-24   **RHYS, JEAN** / After Leaving Mr. Mackenzie

V-42   **RHYS, JEAN** / Good Morning Midnight

V-319   **RHYS, JEAN** / Quartet

V-2016   **ROSEN, KENNETH (ed.)** / The Man to Send Rain Clouds: Contemporary Stories by American Indians

V-976   **ROTHENBERG, JEROME AND GEORGE QUASHA (eds.)** / America a Prophecy: A New Reading of American Poetry From Pre-Columbian Times to the Present

V-41   **SARGENT, PAMELA (ed.)** / Women of Wonder: Science Fiction Stories by Women About Women

V-838   **SARTRE, JEAN-PAUL** / The Age of Reason

V-238   **SARTRE, JEAN-PAUL** / The Condemned of Altona

V-65   **SARTRE, JEAN-PAUL** / The Devil & The Good Lord & Two Other Plays

V-16   **SARTRE, JEAN-PAUL** / No Exit and Three Other Plays

V-839   **SARTRE, JEAN-PAUL** / The Reprieve

V-74   **SARTRE, JEAN-PAUL** / The Trojan Women: Euripides

V-840   **SARTRE, JEAN-PAUL** / Troubled Sleep

V-607   **SCORTIA, THOMAS N. AND GEORGE ZEBROWSKI (eds.)** / Human-Machines: An Anthology of Stories About Cyborgs

V-330   **SHOLOKHOV, MIKHAIL** / And Quiet Flows the Don

V-331   **SHOLOKHOV, MIKHAIL** / The Don Flows Home to the Sea

V-447   **SILVERBERG, ROBERT** / Born With the Dead: Three Novellas About the Spirit of Man

V-945   **SNOW, LOIS WHEELER** / China On Stage

V-133   **STEIN, GERTRUDE** / Autobiography of Alice B. Toklas

V-826   **STEIN, GERTRUDE** / Everybody's Autobiography

V-941   **STEIN, GERTRUDE** / The Geographical History of America

V-797   **STEIN, GERTRUDE** / Ida

V-695   **STEIN, GERTRUDE** / Last Operas and Plays

V-477   **STEIN, GERTRUDE** / Lectures in America

V-153   **STEIN, GERTRUDE** / Three Lives

V-710   **STEIN, GERTRUDE & CARL VAN VECHTEN (ed.)** / Selected Writings of Gertrude Stein

V-20   **STEINER, STAN AND MARIA-THERESA BABIN (eds.)** / Borinquen: An Anthology of Puerto-Rican Literature

V-770   **STEINER, STAN AND LUIS VALDEZ (eds.)** / Aztlan: An Anthology of Mexican-American Literature

V-769   **STEINER, STAN AND SHIRLEY HILL WITT (eds.)** / The Way: An Anthology of American Indian Literature

V-768   **STEVENS, HOLLY (ed.)** / The Palm at the End of the Mind: Selected Poems & A Play by Wallace Stevens

V-278   **STEVENS, WALLACE** / The Necessary Angel

V-896   **SULLIVAN, VICTORIA AND JAMES HATCH (eds.)** / Plays By and About Women

V-63   **SVEVO, ITALO** / Confessions of Zeno

V-178   **SYNGE, J. M.** / Complete Plays

V-601   **TAYLOR, PAUL B. AND W. H. AUDEN (trans.)** / The Elder Edda

V-443   **TROUPE, QUINCY AND RAINER SCHULTE (eds.)** / Giant Talk: An Anthology of Third World Writings

V-770   **VALDEZ, LUIS AND STAN STEINER (eds.)** / Aztlan: An Anthology of Mexican-American Literature

V-710   **VAN VECHTEN, CARL (ed.) AND GERTRUDE STEIN** / Selected Writings of Gertrude Stein

V-870   **WIESEL, ELIE** / Souls on Fire

V-769   **WITT, SHIRLEY HILL AND STAN STEINER (eds.)** / The Way: An Anthology of American Indian Literature

V-2028   **WODEHOUSE, P. G.** / The Code of the Woosters

V-2026   **WODEHOUSE, P. G.** / Leave It to Psmith

V-2027   **WODEHOUSE, P. G.** / Mulliner Nights

V-607   **ZEBROWSKI, GEORGE AND THOMAS N. SCORTIA (eds.)** / Human-Machines: An Anthology of Stories About Cyborgs